W9-BCK-555

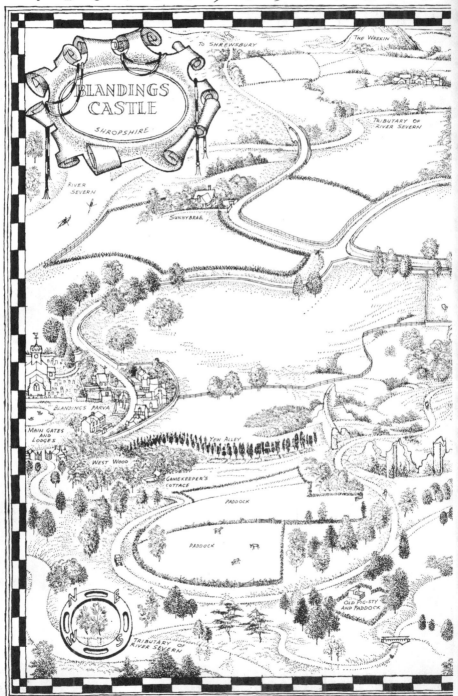

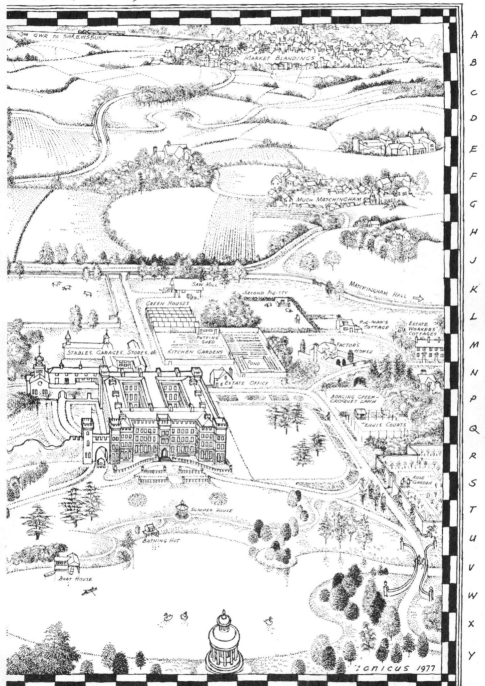

15 16 17 18 19 20 21 22 23 24 25 26 27 28 29

A
B
C
D
E
F
G
H
J
K
L
M
N
P
Q
R
S
T
U
V
W
X
Y

GWR to SHREWSBURY

MARKET BLANDINGS

MUCH MATCHINGHAM

SAW MILL

SECOND PIG-STY

MATCHINGHAM HALL

GREEN HOUSES

PIG-MAN'S COTTAGE

ESTATE WORKERS COTTAGES

POTTING SHED

STABLES, GARAGES, STORES, &c.

KITCHEN GARDENS

POND

FACTOR'S HOUSE

ESTATE OFFICE

BOWLING GREEN — CROQUET LAWN

TENNIS COURTS

ROSE GARDEN

SUMMER HOUSE

BATHING HUT

BOAT HOUSE

IONICUS 1977

OTHER BOOKS BY

The Cat-Nappers
Bachelors Anonymous
The Plot That Thickened
Jeeves and the Tie That Binds
The Girl in Blue
No Nudes Is Good Nudes
Do Butlers Burgle Banks?
Plum Pie
The Purloined Paperweight
The Brinkmanship of Galahad
Threepwood
Biffen's Millions
Stiff Upper Lip, Jeeves
Author! Author!
Service with a Smile
The Ice in the Bedroom
How Right You Are, Jeeves
French Leave
A Few Quick Ones
Cocktail Time
The Butler Did It
America, I Like You

Bertie Wooster Sees It Through
The Return of Jeeves
Pigs Have Wings
Angel Cake
The Old Reliable
Nothing Serious
The Mating Season
Uncle Dynamite
Spring Fever
Full Moon
Joy in the Morning
Money in the Bank
Quick Service
Eggs, Beans and Crumpets
Uncle Fred in the Springtime
The Code of the Woosters
Summer Moonshine
The Crime Wave at Blandings
Laughing Gas
Young Men in Spats
The Luck of the Bodkins
Blandings Castle

P. G. WODEHOUSE

Sunset at Blandings

P. G. WODEHOUSE

WITH NOTES AND APPENDICES BY
RICHARD USBORNE

ILLUSTRATIONS BY IONICUS

SIMON AND SCHUSTER • NEW YORK

Text copyright © 1977 by the Estate of P. G. Wodehouse;
Appendices, Notes and Illustrations copyright © 1977
by Chatto & Windus, Ltd.
All rights reserved
including the right of reproduction
in whole or in part in any form
Published by Simon and Schuster
A Division of Gulf & Western Corporation
Simon and Schuster Building
Rockefeller Center
1230 Avenue of the Americas
New York, New York 10020
Manufactured in the United States of America

1   2   3   4   5   6   7   8   9   10

Library of Congress Cataloging in Publication Data
Wodehouse, Pelham Grenville, 1881-1975.
    Sunset at Blandings.

    I. Usborne, Richard.   II. Title.
PZ3.W817Sv   1978   [PR6045.O53]   823'.9'12   78-2188
ISBN 0-671-24293-8

CONTENTS

ILLUSTRATIONS

SUNSET AT BLANDINGS

CHAPTER ONE

SIR JAMES PIPER, England's Chancellor of the Exchequer, sat in his London study staring before him with what are usually called unseeing eyes and snorting every now and then like somebody bursting a series of small paper bags. Sherlock Holmes, had he seen him, would have deduced instantly that he was not in a good temper.

'Elementary, my dear Watson,' he would have said. 'Those snorts tell the story.'

And Claude Duff, Sir James's junior secretary, who had been intending to ask him if he could have the day off to go and see his aunt at Eastbourne, heard these snorts and changed his mind. He was a nervous young man.

Holmes would have been right. Sir James had been in the worst of humours ever since his sister Brenda had told him that he was to go to Blandings Castle, the Shropshire seat of Clarence, Earl of Emsworth, when he had been planning a fishing holiday in Scotland. And what was worse, he had got to take a girl with him and deliver her to the custody of Lord Emsworth's sister Florence. He disliked modern girls. They were jumpy. They wriggled and giggled. They had no conversation. A long motor journey beside one of them, having to stare at Sergeant Murchison's back all the way, would test him sorely, and not for the first time he found himself wishing that he had a stronger will or, alternatively, that Brenda had a weaker one. Lord Emsworth, that vague and dreamy peer, would have told him that he knew just how he felt. He, too, was a great sufferer from the tyranny of sisters, of whom he had sufficient to equip half a dozen earls.

It was Brenda who had forced James into politics when a distant relative had left him all that money in her will. He had been at the time a happy young lad-about-town wanting nothing but to remain a happy young lad-about-town, but Brenda was adamant. It is said that there is a woman behind every successful man, and never had the statement been proved more remarkably than in the case of young Jimmy Piper.

Today he thoroughly enjoyed politics and the eminence to which he had risen, and he knew that he would never have done it without her behind him with a spiked stick. Often in the early days he had wanted to give the whole thing up — he could still recall with a shudder what a priceless ass he had felt when making his first appearance before the electors of Pudbury-in-the-Vale — but Brenda would have none of it. He supposed he ought to feel grateful to her, and as a rule he did, but when she suddenly produced girls like rabbits out of a hat, gratitude turned to sullen wrath and he felt justified in snorting with even more vehemence.

Brenda came in as he increased the voltage of his eleventh snort, a formidable figure, formidably dressed. Had she been weaker, she might have shown sympathy for the stricken man, but her deportment and words were those of a strong-minded governess who believed in standing no nonsense from a fractious child.

'Oh, really, James, must you make such a crisis of it? You are behaving like an aristocrat of the French Revolution waiting for the tumbril. I'd like to be coming with you, but I can't get away for a day or two. I have that committee meeting.'

If Sir James had been a man of greater mettle, a twelfth snort might have escaped him. As it was, he merely said:

'Who is this girl I'm taking to the castle?'

'Surely I told you?'

'You may have done. I've forgotten.'

'Florence's stepdaughter Victoria. Florence most unwisely let her come to London to study Art, and she has apparently got involved with an impossible young man. Naturally Florence wants her where she can keep an eye on her.'[1]

She had more to say, but at this point a knock on the door interrupted her. There entered a soberly dressed man who gave the impression of having been carved out of some durable kind of wood by a sculptor who had received his tuition from an inefficient tutor. This was Sergeant E. B. Murchison, the detective appointed by the special branch of Scotland Yard to accompany Sir James wherever he went and see to it that he came to no harm from the terror by night and the arrow that flieth by day. He said:

'The car is at the door, Sir James.'[2]

Sir James made no reply, and Brenda answered for him with a gracious 'Thank you, Sergeant'. He withdrew, and Sir James looked after him in a manner most unsuitable towards an honest helper who was prepared, if necessary, to die in his defence.

'God, how I hate that man,' he muttered.

It was the sort of remark which called out all the governess in Brenda. Her face, always on the stony side, grew stonier. It was as though Sir James had kicked the furniture or refused to eat his rice pudding.

'Don't be childish, James.'

'Who's being childish?'

'You're being childish. You have no reason whatever to dislike Sergeant Murchison.'

'Haven't I? How would you like being followed around wherever you go? How would you enjoy being dogged from morning to night by a man who makes you feel as if you were someone wanted by the police because they think you may be able to assist them in their enquiries? I expect daily, when I take a bath, to find Murchison nestling in the soap dish.'

Miss Piper had no patience with these tantrums.

'My dear James, a man in your position has to have protection.'

'Why? What's he supposed to be protecting me *from*? Is Blandings Castle the den of the Secret Nine? Is Emsworth a modern Macbeth? Is he going to creep into my room at night with a dagger? And if he does, how can that blasted Murchison protect me? How can he stop anyone assassinating me if he's snoring his repulsive head off a quarter of a mile away? Or will he be sleeping on the mat outside my door? I don't know what you're laughing at,' said Sir James with *hauteur*, for Brenda's face had softened into an amused smile.

'I was picturing Lord Emsworth as a modern Macbeth.'

Sir James had thought of something else to complain about.

'Shall I be plunging into the middle of a large party? Public dinners are bad enough, but big country house parties are worse. I always used to hate them, even as a young man.'

'Of course it won't be a large party. Just Florence and her sister Diana Phipps. What on earth's the matter, James?' said Brenda petulantly, for Sir James had leaped like one of the trout he was so fond of catching. His eyes were gleaming with a strange light and he had to gulp before he could speak.

'Nothing's the matter.'

'You jumped.'

'You surprised me, saying that Diana Phipps was at Blandings. I thought she lived in East Africa.'

'You know her?'

'I used to know her ages ago. Before,' said Sir James,

and he spoke bitterly, 'she chucked herself away on that ass Rollo[3] Phipps.'

'I always heard he was very attractive.'

'If you call looking like a film star attractive. Not a brain in his head. Spent all his time shooting big game. My God!' said Sir James with sudden alarm, 'There's no danger of him being at Blandings?'

'Not unless he is haunting the castle. He was killed by a lion years ago.'

'And nobody told me!'

'Why should anyone tell you?'

'Because . . . because I would have liked to extend my sympathy to Diana.'

One of the gifts which go to make up the type of super-women to whom Brenda belonged is the ability to read faces. Brenda had it in full measure, especially where her brother was concerned.

'James!' Her voice was at its keenest. 'Were you in love with her?'

It might have been supposed that a man of Sir James's long experience as a Cabinet minister would have replied 'I must have notice of that question', but excitement precluded caution. His mind was in a ferment and had flitted back to the days before he had come into all that money and gone into politics, the days when he had been plain Jimmy Piper, longing to make an impression on lovely Diana Threepwood but always tongue-tied, always elbowed to one side by the fellows with the gift of the gab. It was only later, gradually rising on stepping-stones of his dead self to higher things, that he had acquired the politician's ability to use a great many words when saying nothing.

'Of course I was in love with her,' he replied with defiance. 'We were all in love with her. And she went and threw herself away on Rollo Phipps.'

'Well, he's dead now.'

'Yes, that's something.'

'And she's at Blandings.'

'Yes.'

'And you're going to Blandings.'

'Yes.'

'You're probably glad of it now.'

'Yes.'

'You intend to ask her to marry you?'

'Yes.'

'It would be an excellent thing for both of you.'

'Yes.'

'But there is one thing I must warn you about. I have never met Diana, but if she is anything like the other Threepwood girls, she abominates weakness.'[4]

'I'm not weak.'

'You're shy, which can quite easily give that impression. So when you propose, don't stammer and yammer. Be firm. Dominate her. Otherwise she won't look at you.'

'I'll remember.'

'Mind you do. Those girls abominate weakness.'

'You said that before.'

'And I say it again. Look at Florence and her husband.'

'I always thought Underwood was one of those steel and iron American millionaires.'

'Her second husband. Underwood died, and she married a man who couldn't say Bo to a goose.'

'Very rude of him if he did, unless he knew the goose very well.'

'That's why Florence and her husband are separated.'

'They are, are they?'

'He's weak. You wouldn't think it to look at him, because he's one of those extraordinary virile men in appearance. If you can imagine a Greek god with a small clipped moustache . . . You had better be starting, James. You heard Sergeant Murchison say the car was waiting.'

'Let it wait. You don't know who else will be at Blandings do you?'

'No, Florence didn't say.'

'I was wondering if Gally would be there.'

'Who?'

'Galahad Threepwood.'

'I sincerely hope not,' said Brenda.

Like the majority of his sisters, she thoroughly disapproved of Lord Emsworth's younger brother.

'Do you see anything of Galahad Threepwood nowadays?' she asked suspiciously.

'Haven't seen him for years. We were great friends in the old days.'

The snort which proceeded from Brenda might not have been a snort of the calibre of those which her brother had emitted, but it was definitely a sniff. The subject of the old days was one normally avoided by both of them — on his part from caution, on hers because the mere thought of those days revolted her. She preferred not to be reminded that there had been a time, before she took charge of him, when James had moved in a most undesirable circle — a member in fact of the Pelican Club[5] to which Galahad Threepwood had belonged.

'I believe he has a prison record,' she said.

Sir James hastened to correct this hasty statement.

'No, he was always given the option of a fine.'

'You are keeping the car waiting,' said Brenda coldly.

CHAPTER TWO

JNO ROBINSON'S taxi,[6] which meets all the trains
at Market Blandings, drew up with a screeching of brakes
at the great door of Blandings Castle, and a dapper little
man of the type one automatically associates in one's
mind with white bowler hats and race glasses bumping
against the left hip alighted with the agile abandon of a
cat on hot bricks. This was Lord Emsworth's brother
Galahad, and he moved briskly at all times because he
always felt so well. He was too elderly to be rejoicing in
his youth, but he gave the impression of rejoicing in
something.

A niece of his had once commented on this.

'It really is an extraordinary thing,' she had said, 'that
anyone who has had such a good time as he has can be so
frightfully healthy. Everywhere you look you see men
leading model lives and pegging out in their prime, but
good old Uncle Gally, who apparently never went to bed
till he was fifty, is still breezing along as fit and rosy as
ever.'

Galahad Threepwood was the only genuinely dis-
tinguished member of the family of which Lord Emsworth was the head. Lord Emsworth himself had once
won a first prize for pumpkins at the Shropshire Agricultural Show, and his Berkshire sow, Empress of
Blandings, had three times been awarded the silver medal
for fatness, but you could not say that he had really risen
to eminence in the public life of England. But Gally
had made a name for himself. There were men in London
—bookmakers, skittle sharps, jellied eel sellers on race

18

courses, and men like that—who would not have known whom you were referring to if you had mentioned Einstein, but they all knew Gally. He had been, till that institution passed beyond the veil, a man at whom the old Pelican Club pointed with pride, and had known more policemen by their first names than any man in the metropolis.[7]

After paying and tipping Jno Robinson and enquiring after his wife, family and rheumatism, for in addition to being fit and rosy he had a heart which was not only of gold but in the right place, he made his way to the butler's pantry, eager after his absence in London to get in touch with Sebastian Beach, for eighteen years the castle's major domo. He and Beach had been firm friends since, as he put it, they were kids of forty.

Beach welcomed him with respectful fervour and produced port for which after his long train journey he was pining, and for a while all was quiet except for the butler's bullfinch,[8] crooning meditatively to itself in its cage on the window sill. The sort of port you got in Beach's pantry if you were as old a friend as Gally was did not immediately encourage conversation, but had to be sipped in reverent silence. Eventually Gally spoke. Having uttered an enthusiastic 'Woof!' in appreciation of the elixir, he said:

'Well, Beach, let's have all the news. How's Clarence?'

'His lordship is in good health, Mr. Galahad.'

'And the Empress?'

'Extremely robust.'

'Clarence still hanging on her lightest word?'

'His lordship's affection has suffered no diminution.'

'Of course it wouldn't have. I keep forgetting that it's only a week since I was here.'[9]

'Was it agreeable in London, sir?'

'Not very. Have you ever noticed, Beach, how your views change as the years go by?[10] There was a time when

19

you had to employ wild horses to drag me from London, and they had to spit on their hands and make a special effort. And now I can't stand the place. Gone to the dogs since they did away with hansom cabs and spats. Do you realize that not a single leg in London has got a spat on it today?'

'Very sad, sir.'

'A tragedy. Except for an occasional binge like the annual dinner of the Loyal Sons of Shropshire, which was what took me up there this time, I have shaken the dust of London from my feet. I shall settle down at Blandings and grow a long white beard. The great thing about Blandings is that it never changes. When you come back to it after a temporary absence, you don't find they've built on a red-brick annexe to the left wing and pulled down a couple of the battlements. A spot more of the true and blushful, Beach.'

'Certainly, Mr. Galahad.'

'Of course one sees new faces. Pig men come and go. The boy who cleans the knives and boots is not always the same. Dogs die and maids marry. And, arising from that, who was the girl I passed on my way through the hall? She reminded me of someone I knew in the old days who used to dive off roofs into tanks of water. Daredevil Esmeralda she called herself. She subsequently married a man in the hay, corn and feed business. Who is this girl? Blue eyes and brown hair. She's new to me.'

'That would be her ladyship's maid, Marilyn Poole, Mr. Galahad.'

'Ladyship? What ladyship?'

'Lady Diana,'[11] sir.'

Galahad, who had started and stiffened at the word 'ladyship', drew a relieved breath. He was very fond of his sister Diana, the only one of his many sisters with whom he was on cordial terms. When he had left the castle, it had been a purely male establishment, Lord

Emsworth and himself its only occupants; and though he
would have preferred it to remain so, if it was only Diana
who had muscled in, he had no complaints to make. It
might so easily have been Hermione or Dora or Julia or
Florence.

'So Lady Diana's here, is she?' he said.

'Yes, sir. She arrived shortly after Lady Florence.'

Gally's monocle fell from his eye.

'You aren't telling me *Florence* is here?' he quavered.

'Yes, Mr. Galahad. Also her stepdaughter, Miss
Victoria Underwood.'

Gally was a resilient man. His monocle might have
become detached from the parent eye at the news that
Blandings Castle housed his sister Florence, but this
further piece of information did much to restore his
customary euphoria. Florence, widow of the wealthy
J. B. Underwood, the American millionaire, might be a
depressant, but his niece Vicky's company he always
enjoyed.

'How was she?' he asked.

'Her ladyship seemed much as usual.'

'Not Lady Florence. Vicky.'

'Somewhat depressed, I thought.'

'I must cheer her up.'

'Sir James Piper is also a guest.'

This final news item brought a further ray of sunshine to Gally's mood. Only the fear of choking on
Beach's superb port prevented him uttering a glad
cry.

'Old Jimmy Piper!' he said when he was at liberty to
speak. 'I haven't seen him for years. I used to know him
well. Sad how time ruins old friendships. What is he now?
Prime Minister or something, isn't he?'

'Chancellor of the Exchequer, sir, I understand.'

'He's come on a lot since we were fellow members of
the Pelican. I remember young Jimmy Piper used

constantly to be chucked out of the old Gardenia.[5] I suppose he's had to give up all that sort of thing now. That's the curse of getting to the top in politics. You lose your *joie de vivre*. I don't suppose Jimmy has been thrown out of a restaurant for years. But mark you, Beach, he is more to be pitied than censured. Just as he was at his best a ghastly sister came to live with him and changed his whole outlook. That's why we drifted apart. I looked him up one day, all agog for one of our customary frolics, and the sister was there and she froze me stiff. We could have met at his club, of course, in fact he asked me to lunch there, but when I found that his club was the Athenaeum, crawling, as you probably know, with bishops and no hope of anyone throwing bread at anyone, I bowed out. And I've not seen him since. The right thing to do, don't you think? Making a clean cut of it. The surgeon's knife. But it will be delightful seeing Jimmy again. I hope he hasn't brought his sister with him.'

'He has, Mr. Galahad.'

'What!'

'Or, rather, Miss Piper is expected in a few days.'

'Oh, my God! Does Clarence know?'

'His lordship has been informed.'

'How did he take it?'

'He appeared somewhat disturbed.'

'I don't wonder. Blandings Castle seems to be filling up like the Black Hole of Calcutta, and a single guest gives him a sinking feeling. Where is he?'

'At the Empress's sty, I presume, Mr. Galahad.'

'I must go to him immediately and do my best to console him. A pretty figure I should cut in the eyes of posterity if I were to sit here swilling port while my only brother was up to his collar stud in the Slough of Despond.'

And so saying Gally leaped to the door.

He had scarcely reached the outer air when a small but

solid body flung itself into his arms with a squeal of welcome. Victoria (Vicky) Underwood was always glad to see her Uncle Galahad, and never more so than at a time when, as Beach had said, she was somewhat depressed.

CHAPTER THREE

UNCLES occasionally find their nephews trying and are inclined to compare them to their disadvantage with the young men they knew when they were young men, but it is a very rare uncle who is unable to fraternize with his nieces. And of all his many nieces Gally was fondest of Vicky. She was pretty, a girl whom it was a pleasure to take to race meetings and garden parties, and she had that animation which in his younger days he had found so attractive in music hall artistes and members of the personnel of the chorus.[12]

This animation was missing now. After that tempestuous greeting she had relapsed into a melancholy which would have entitled her to step straight into one of those sombre plays they put on for one performance on Sunday afternoons, and no questions asked. Gally gazed at her, concerned. Beach, that shrewd diagnostician, had been right, he felt, though his 'somewhat depressed' had been an understatement. Here was plainly a niece whose soul had been passed through the wringer, a niece who had drained the bitter cup and, what is more, had found a dead mouse at the bottom of it. Her demeanour reminded him of a girl he had once taken to Henley Regatta — at the moment when she had discovered that a beetle had fallen down the back of her summer sports wear.

'What on earth's the matter?' he asked.

'Nothing.'

'Don't be an ass,' said Gally irritably. 'You're obviously as down among the wines and spirits as Mariana at the moated grange.'

24

'I'm all right, except that I wish I was dead.'

'Were dead, surely,' said Gally, who was a purist. 'What do you want to be dead for? Great Scott!' he exclaimed, suddenly enlightened. 'Have you been jugged? Are you doing a stretch? Is that why you're at Blandings?'

The question did not display such amazing intuition as anyone unfamiliar with Blandings Castle might have supposed. All old English families have their traditions, and the one most rigorously observed in the family to which Vicky belonged ruled that if a young female member of it fell in love with the wrong man she was instantly shipped off to Blandings, there to remain until she came, as the expression was, to her senses.

Young male members who fell in love with the wrong girls were sent to South Africa, as Gally had been thirty years ago. It was all rather unpleasant for the lovelorn juveniles, but better than if they had been living in the Middle Ages, when they would probably have had their heads cut off.

Gally, taking for granted that the reply to his question would be in the affirmative, became reminiscent.

'Lord love a duck,' he said emotionally, 'it seems only yesterday that they had me serving a term in the lowest dungeon below the castle moat because of Dolly Henderson.'[13]

Feminine curiosity momentarily overcame Vicky's depression. She knew vaguely that there had been some sort of trouble with Uncle Gally centuries ago, and she was glad to be about to get the facts.

'Were you imprisoned at Blandings?'

'With gyves upon my wrists.'

'I thought you were sent to South Africa.'

'Later, after I had been well gnawed by rats.'

'Who was Dolly Henderson?'

'Music halls. She sang at the old Oxford and the Tivoli.'

'Tights?'

'Pink. And she was the only woman I ever wanted to marry.'

'Poor Gally.'

'Yes, it was rather a nasty knock when my father bunged a spanner into the works. You never knew him, did you?'

'I met him once when I was a very small child. He paralysed me.'

'I don't wonder. That voice, those bushy eyebrows. You must have thought you were seeing some sinister monster out of a fairy story.[14] Clarence is a great improvement as head of the family. If I told Clarence I wanted to marry somebody, there wouldn't be any family curses and thumping of tables; he would just say "Capital, capital, capital", and that would be that. But don't let's talk about me. Are you very much in love?'

'Yes.'

'What's his name?'

'Jeff Bennison.'

'Any money?'

'No.'

'Which of course makes your stepmother shudder at the sight of him.'

'She's never seen him.'

'But she would shudder if she did. Lack of the stuff is always the rock on which the frail craft of love comes a stinker where Blandings Castle is concerned.'

'And there's another thing.'

'What is that?'

'Jeff's an artist.'

Gally looked grave. To his sister Florence, he knew, an artist would be automatically suspect. *La vie de Bohème*, she would say to herself. Uninhibited goings-on at the Bohemian Ball. Nameless orgies in the old studio. Now more than ever he saw how grievously the cards were

26

stacked against this young couple, and his heart went out to them.

'He started as an architect, but his father lost all his money and he couldn't carry on. So he tried to make a living painting, but you know how it is. Poor darling, he has had to take a job teaching drawing at a girls' school.'

'Good God!'

'Yes, I think that's how he feels about it. Do you mind if I leave you now, Gally? I feel a flood of tears coming on.'

'I am open at the moment to be cried in front of.'

'No, I'd rather be alone.'

'I'm sorry. I was hoping I could do something to cheer you up. But naturally at a time like this you don't want an old gargoyle like me hanging around.'

Gally proceeded on his way, brooding. He would have given much to have been able to do something to brighten life for the unfortunate girl, but no inspiration came beyond a vague determination to speak to his sister Florence like a Dutch uncle, and he was given the opportunity of doing this as he crossed the lawn which led to the Empress's residence. Florence was there, reading a book in the hammock under the big cedar tree which he, though there was no actual ruling on the point, had always looked on as his own property. Many of his deepest thoughts had come to him when on its cushions, and it was with a sense of outrage that he drew up beside it. If people went about pinching one's personal hammock, he felt, what were things coming to?

'Comfortable?' he said.

Florence looked up from her book, expressing no pleasure at seeing him.

'Oh, you're back, Galahad? Did you enjoy yourself in London?'

'Never mind about my enjoying myself in London,' said Gally as sternly as any uncle that ever came out of Holland. 'I've just been talking to Vicky.'

'Oh?'

'She's upset.'

'Oh?'

'Crying buckets, poor child.'

'Oh?'

'She tells me you object to this dream man of hers.'

'I do. Very strongly.'

'Although you've never seen him. Just because he's short of money. As if everybody wasn't nowadays except Clarence and you. Your late husband must have left you enough to sink a ship. Didn't he leave Vicky any?'

'He did. I'm the trustee for it.'

'And sitting on it like a buzzard on a rock, I gather. What's wrong with this fellow she wants to marry? Is he a criminal of some kind?'

'Probably. His father was.'

'What do you mean?'

'Didn't she tell you his name?'

'Jeff something.'

'Bennison. His father was Arthur Bennison.'

'So what?'

'Have you never heard of Arthur Bennison? It was the great sensation years ago.'

'I must have been out of England. What did he do? Murder somebody?'

'No, just swindled all the people who had invested in his companies. My first husband was one of them. He left the country to avoid arrest and took refuge in one of those South American republics where they don't have extradition. He died five years ago. So now perhaps you can see why I don't want Victoria to marry his son.'

Gally shook his head.

'I don't get it. Is that all you've got against him?'

'Isn't it enough?'

'Not from where I sit. You might just as well refuse to associate with yourself because you had a father like ours.'

'Father was a bully and a tyrant, but he didn't swindle people.'

'Probably because he didn't think of it. As a matter of fact, you know perfectly well that swindling fathers have nothing to do with your objection to Vicky's young man. What gashes you like a knife is his being short of cash. You're a hard woman, Florence. What you need are a few quarts of the milk of human kindness. Look at the way you're treating that husband of yours. Driving him out into the snow and bringing his clipped moustache in sorrow to the grave. Who do you think you are? *La belle dame sans merci* or something?'

Florence picked up her book.

'Oh, go away, Galahad. You're impossible.'

'Just off. I can't bring you another cushion?'

'No, thanks.'

'I've heard it said that lying in a hammock is bad for the spine.'

'Who did you hear it said by?'

'A doctor at the Pelican Club.'

'I suppose all members of the Pelican Club were half-witted.'

Gally withdrew. He was thinking as he resumed his search for his brother Clarence that talking like a Dutch uncle to somebody was all right unless that somebody happened to be a Dutch aunt.

CHAPTER FOUR

HE FOUND Lord Emsworth, as he had expected, drooping over the Empress's sty like a wet sock and gazing at its occupant with a rapt expression.

His devotion to the silver medallist had long been the occasion for adverse comment from his nearest and dearest. His severest critic, his sister Constance, was now in America, but there were others almost equally out-spoken.

'Old girl,' his brother-in-law Colonel Wedge had said on one occasion to his wife Hermione, returning late at night from a visit to London, 'we've got to face it, Clarence is dotty. Where do you think I found him just now? Down at the pig sty. I noticed something hanging over the rail and thought the pig man must have left his overalls there, and then it suddenly reared itself up and said "Ah, Egbert". Gave me a nasty shock. Questioned as to what he was doing there at that time of night, he said he was listening to his pig.[15] And what, you will ask, was the pig doing? Singing? Reciting "Dangerous Dan McGrew"? Nothing of the kind. Just breathing.'

Nor had Gally, fond though he was of his brother, abstained from criticism.

'I have been closely associated with Clarence for more than half a century, and I know him from caviare to nuts,' had been his verdict. 'His I.Q. is about thirty points lower than that of a not too agile-minded jellyfish. Capital chap, though. One of the best.'

As Gally approached, he peered at him with a puzzled look on his face, as if he knew he had seen him before somewhere, but could not think where. With an effort he identified him and gave him a brotherly nod.

'Ah, Galahad.'

'Ah to you, Clarence, with knobs on.'

'You're here, eh?'

'Yes, right here.'

'Someone told me you had gone to London.'

'I've come back.'

'Come back. I see. Come back, you mean. Yes, quite. What did you go to London for?'

'Primarily to attend the Loyal Sons of Shropshire dinner. But I heard that a pal of mine was in a nursing home with a broken leg, so I stayed on to cheer him up.'

'Nasty thing, a broken leg.'

'Yes, it annoyed Stiffy a good deal.'

'It was he who broke his leg?'

'Yes. Friend of mine from the old Pelican days. Stiffy Bates.'

'How did he break his leg?'

'Getting off an omnibus.'

'He should have taken a cab.'

'Yes, he'll know better next time.'

They brooded in silence for a while their thoughts busy with the ill-starred Stiffy. Then Gally, though nothing could be more enjoyable than this exchange of ideas on the subject of broken legs, felt that it was time for the condolences which he had come to deliver. Stiffy Bates might have his leg in plaster, but how much more in need of cheering up was a man who would shortly have Jimmy Piper's sister Brenda staying with him.

'And while I was cheering Stiffy up, I ran into Kevin and had to cheer him up too. I was busy for days.'

'Who is Kevin?'

'Come, come, Clarence, this is not worthy of your lightning brain. Kevin Moresby, Florence's husband.'

The words 'Who is Florence?' trembled on Lord

Emsworth's lips, but he was able to choke them back and substitute 'And why did Kevin need cheering up?'

'Because he and Florence are separated. She has cast him off like a used tube of toothpaste, and he doesn't like it. I don't know why,' Gally added, for it was his private opinion that Kevin was in luck.

'I never approved of that marriage,' said Lord Emsworth.

'It was entirely unexpected.'

'Most.'

It was about a year since Florence, left a widow by the death of J. B. Underwood, and inheriting from him several million dollars, had startled a good many people by marrying the very handsome but impoverished Kevin Moresby, referred to in the press as 'the playwright'. Kevin was one of those dramatists who start when very young with a colossal hit and cannot repeat. His last seven plays had been failures, and Florence's money had been a welcome windfall. It was easy to imagine what a blow their separation must have been to him.

'Married her for her money, I've always thought,' said Lord Emsworth.

'The same idea occurred to me,' said Gally.

'This is grave news,' he continued, 'about Jimmy Piper's sister.'

'Who is Jimmy Piper?'

'He's staying here.'

'Ah yes, I think I may have seen him. Has he a sister?'

'Yes, and . . . Haven't you heard?'

'Not to my recollection. What about her?'

On the point of answering the question, Gally paused. His brother, he perceived, had completely forgotten what he had been told about the Brenda menace. It was his custom to forget in a matter of minutes anything said to him. It would not be humane, Gally felt, to spoil his day by refreshing his memory. Let him be happy while he could.

'I can't remember,' he said. 'Somebody told me something about her but it's slipped my mind. The Empress looks as fit as ever,' he added, to change the subject.

'She is in wonderful health.'

'Eating well?'

'Magnificently. It's too bad that I can't get anyone to paint her portrait.[16] I did think it would be plain sailing when Connie went to America, but all the prominent artists I have approached have refused the commission.'

To add a likeness of the Empress to those of his ancestors in the Blandings Castle portrait gallery had long been Lord Emsworth's dream, and with the departure of his sister Constance, the spearhead of the movement in opposition to the scheme, his hopes had risen high. The difficulty was to find a suitable artist. All the leading Royal Academicians to whom he had applied had informed him rather stiffly that they did not paint pigs. They painted sheep in Scottish glens, children playing with kittens and puppies, still-life representations of oranges and bananas on plates, but not pigs.

Gally had always approved of the idea, arguing that the Empress could not but lend tone to a gallery filled with the ugliest collection of thugs he had ever had the misfortune to see, comparable only to the Chamber of Horrors at Madame Tussaud's. He made but one exception, the sixth Earl, who he said reminded him of a charming pea and thimble man with whom he had formed a friendship one afternoon at Hurst Park race course the year Billy Buttons won the Jubilee Cup.

'They were very firm about it,' said Lord Emsworth. 'Some of them were quite rude.'

'Egad!' said Gally.

'Eh?' said Lord Emsworth.

'Just egad, Clarence. I've had an inspiration.'

At the word 'portrait' a close observer would have noticed a sudden sparkle in the eye behind Gally's black-rimmed monocle. This usually happened when he got a bright idea.

'Why waste time on Royal Academicians?' he said. 'A lot of stuffed shirts. You don't need what you call a prominent artist. You want an eager young fellow all vim and ginger, and I've got the very man for you. He specializes in pigs.'

'You don't say, Galahad! What's his name?'

'You wouldn't know his name.'

'Is he good?'

'I believe his morals are excellent.'

'At painting, I mean.'

'Terrific.'

'Is he very expensive?'

'He won't charge you a penny. He is very well off, and only paints pigs because he loves them.'

'Is he free at the moment?'

'That is what I shall ascertain when I run up to London tomorrow.'

'My dear Galahad, you can't run up to London to-morrow. You only came back today.'

'What of that? If a man can't run up to London because he has just run down from it, where can he run up to? I want to do you a good turn.'

'It's extremely kind of you, Galahad.'

'Just my old boy scout training, Clarence. One never quite loses the urge to do one's daily good deed.'

Gally walked back to Vicky.

'I think I'll run up to London and interview this young man of yours, to see if he's worthy of you. What's his name besides Jeff?'

'Bennison. But you'll have to run further than London. His school's at Eastbourne.'

'Odd how these schools all flock to the east coast.[17] It's like one of those great race movements of the Middle Ages. Were you at Eastbourne?'

'Yes, at Dame Daphne Winkworth's,[18] only she wasn't a Dame then. That's where Jeff is.'

'Oh my God. I hope I don't run into her. She was a guest at Blandings not long ago, and our relations were none too cordial. It would be embarrassing to meet her again. But I'll risk it for your sake.'

'What an angel you are, Gally. I'll give you a letter to take to Jeff. My correspondence is closely watched.'

'So was mine. It's the first move of the prison authorities.'

CHAPTER FIVE

THANKS to the absence of his employer Claude Duff had got the day off and was on his way to the fashionable girls' school outside Eastbourne to pay his respects to his aunt Dame Daphne Winkworth, its proprietress. His journey had been uneventful and would not merit attention but for the fact that he happened to share a compartment with Gally, who soon established cordial relations with him. Gally was always a great talker to strangers on trains.

Claude was tall and as aggressively good looking as a film-star. His clothes were impeccable, for he was particular about the way he looked. At school, where he had shared a study with Jeff Bennison, he had always been pained by the casualness of the latter's costume. When visiting his aunt, he took especial pains to have everything just right, and he was flicking a speck of dust off his left trouser leg when there came out of the front door a stalwart young man, the sight of whom caused him to stare, to blink, and finally to utter a glad cry of 'Bingo!'

It was an embarrassing moment for Jeff. He recognized his old schoolmate without difficulty, but he had no recollection of what his nickname was. And when an old friend has hailed you as 'Bingo', you cannot be formal. He compromised by calling Claude nothing. So when Claude said he was blowed and that Jeff was the last chap he had expected to see coming out of a girls' school, he merely replied that he worked there.

'You work here? How do you mean?'

'I teach drawing.'

'Somebody told me you were an architect.'

'I had to give it up. No money.'

'Oh, I say! That's too bad.'

'Just one of those things. What are you doing now?'

'I'm second secretary to Sir James Piper.'

'The name seems familiar.'

'Chancellor of the Exchequer.'

'Golly, you're moving in exalted circles. How do you like your job?'

'Very much. How do you like teaching drawing?'

'I don't like it. Or didn't. Recently—in fact this morning—I have been relieved of my duties.'

'Eh?'

'Sacked. Fired. Given the push. I had a dispute with the boss and lost my temper.'

'Gosh! Aunt Daphne wouldn't like that.'

'She didn't. So she's your aunt, is she?'

'Yes.'

'Sooner you than me.'

'What will you do now?'

'Look around, I suppose, till I find something worthy of my talents. But I mustn't stand talking to you. I must go and finish my packing. She wants me off the place at my earliest convenience. Or sooner.'

Left alone, Claude stood musing. He was a goodhearted young man, and Jeff's predicament had saddened him. He himself had never had to worry about money. His father had pushed him into this secretarial job, thinking it would lead to all sorts of things—if he wanted to go into Parliament, for instance—but if Sir James ever decided to part company with him he had several rich relations ready to give him employment. But Jeff who had been his hero at school . . . he didn't like the look of Jeff's position at all.

He was still brooding and was liking the position less than ever, when the dapper little man he had met on the

37

train came trotting up.[19] Glad of anything which would divert his gloomy thoughts, he greeted him effusively, and the little man seemed equally pleased to see him.

'We meet again,' he said. 'Did I finish that story of mine about my friend Fruity Biffen and the Assyrian beard? I fancy not. It was one he bought at Clarkson's in order to be able to attend the Spring meeting at Newmarket and at the same time avoid recognition from the various bookies he owed money to. And he was just passing the stall of Tim Simms, the Safe Man, when it fell off. Something wrong with the gum, one supposes.'

'Was Simms one of the ones he owed money to?'

'One of the many, and there was a painful scene. But Fruity's life was never what you would call placid. I remember one morning asking him to come for a walk in the park with me. It was at the epoch when I was rather addicted to feeding the ducks on the Serpentine. He was horrified. "Me out of doors on a Monday in the daytime!" he gasped. "You must be mad. If only Duff and Trotter will trust me for a couple of raised pies[20] and a case of old brandy, I intend hiding in the crypt of St. Paul's till the bookies have forgotten all about the City and Suburban." Did you tell me, by the way, that your name was Duff?'

'That's right.'

'Any relation to Duff and Trotter, the provision people?'

'My uncle.'

'Then you ought to be all right for raised pies. Galahad Threepwood at this end. Do you come to this seminary often?'

'Fairly often.'

'Then perhaps you can help me. How do I find a fellow called Bennison?'

Claude was all animation.

'Jeff Bennison? Old Bingo? I've just been talking to him. One of my oldest friends.'

'Really?'

'He's gone up to his room.'

'Then I will follow him.'

Jeff, his packing finished, had left his room. Dame Daphne's butler met him at the foot of the stairs.

'There is a gentleman to see you, Mr. Bennison,' he said. 'I have shown him to the morning room.'

Gally was polishing his eyeglass when Jeff joined him in the morning room, as always when ill at ease. He was not a man to be readily unnerved, but even he quailed a little now that he was in such close proximity to Dame Daphne Winkworth.

'Mr. Bennison?' he said. 'How do you do. My name is Threepwood. You must pardon me for being agitated.'

'You don't seem agitated to me.'

'I wear the mask, do I? I am agitated, though. I am in the position of a native of India who knows that a tigress is lurking in the undergrowth near at hand and wonders how soon she will be among those present. I allude to Dame Daphne Winkworth. No danger of her dropping in, is there?'

'I shouldn't think so.'

'Good. Then we can proceed. I come bringing a letter from my niece Victoria. I am her Uncle Galahad.'

'Oh, how do you do?' said Jeff. 'I've heard her talk of you.'

'No doubt she has a fund of good stories. Here's the letter.'

'You don't mind if I kiss it?'

'I shall be offended if you don't.'

'And if I then skim through it for a moment?'

'Go ahead.'

It was some little time before Jeff was able to resume the conversation.

'Thank God you brought me this,' he said at length.
'I've been worrying myself into a decline. I kept writing
to her, but no answer.'

'I doubt if she got your letters.'

'I sent them to her London address.'

'Then they were probably forwarded to Blandings
Castle, where she now is, and intercepted and destroyed.
I'd better sketch out for you the position of affairs concerning you and Vicky and the Blandings Castle circle.
Finding out about your romance, my sister Florence
instantly had Vicky arrested and hauled off to the clink.
In other words, she was taken to Blandings. This, I may
say, is always done when girls of my family fall in love
with men whom their mothers consider undesirable. It's a
matter of money, of course. Unless the chap has a solid
balance at the bank, he automatically become undesirable.
You, I gather from Vicky, have nothing but your salary
here.'

'Not even that. I've just been fired.'

'Really? Too bad.'

'A merciful release I looked on it as. The thought that I
shall never have to see another school-girl trying to draw
is like a tonic. Of course, the situation has its disadvantages.
I expect to starve in the gutter at any moment.'

'No money?'

'Very little.'

'No prospects?'

'Only hopes. It's like this. If you're Vicky's Uncle
Galahad, you must be my friend Freddie Threepwood's
Uncle Galahad.'

'Remorselessly true, but I don't see where you're
heading.'

'I mean you know all about Freddie,[21] that he's out in
America selling dog-biscuits and has become a regular
tycoon and knows everybody — editors and people like
that.'

'I believe he's doing very well. He took the precaution of starting his career by marrying the boss's daughter.'

'He was in England not long ago. They sent him over to buck up the English end of the business.'

Gally, who, like all confirmed *raconteurs*, was not good at listening patiently to other people's stories, heaved a sigh.

'I'm sure this narrative is getting somewhere,' he said, 'but I wish you would tell me where.'

'I'm coming to the nub. The last time he was in England I gave him a comic strip I'd done to try to sell to some paper over there. You know those comic strips — Mutt and Jeff, Blondie, all that. They go on for ever, and it means big money. I'll be on velvet if he sells it.'

'He's bound to. There are no limits to the powers of a man capable of selling dog-biscuits. But meanwhile you will probably be glad of a job to keep you from starving in that gutter you spoke of.'

'I certainly would.'

'Then listen carefully and I'll tell you how this can be arranged.'

Whatever Gally's defects — and someone like his sister Hermione[22] could speak of these by the hour, scarcely pausing to take in breath — he could tell a story well, and long before the conclusion of his résumé of recent events at Blandings Castle, Jeff had gathered that he was to become the latest of the long line of impostors who had sneaked into that stately home of England.

'You have no objection to becoming an impostor?'[23]

'I shall enjoy it.'

'I felt sure you would say so. One can see at a glance that you have the same spirit of adventure that animated Drake, Stanley, and Doctor Livingstone and is the motive power of practically all cats. You'll like Blandings. Gravel soil, company's own water, extensive views over charming old-world parkland. You will, moreover, be constantly in the society of my brother Clarence and his monumental pig, which alone is worth the price of admission. And now think of a name.'

'For me?'

'It would hardly be within the sphere of practical politics to use your own, considering that my sister Florence writhes like an electric eel at the very sound of it. David Lloyd-George? Good, but still not quite what we want. Messmore Breamworthy?'

'Could there be a name like that?'

'It is the name of one of Freddie's co-workers at Donaldson's Dog Joy, Long Island City, U.S.A. But I don't really like it. Too ornate, and the same objection holds in the case of Aubrey Trefusis, Alexander Strong-in-th'-Arm and Augustus Cave-Brown-Cave. We need something simple, easily remembered. Wibberley-Smith? I like the Smith. We'll settle on that. Bless my soul,' said Gally with fervour, 'how it brings back old triumphs, this sketching out plans for adding another impostor to the Blandings roll of honour. But the thing has rather lost its tang since Connie went to America. The man who could introduce an impostor into the castle under Connie's X-ray eye and keep him there undetected had done something he could be proud of. "This," he could say to himself, "was my finest hour!" '

CHAPTER SIX

THE JOURNEY from Eastbourne to Market Blandings is a long and tiring one, but Gally's wiry frame was
more than equal to it, and he alighted at his destination
in good shape. He was, however, afflicted by a thirst
which could not wait to be slaked by Beach's port, and he
made his way to the Emsworth Arms[24] for a beaker of the
celebrated beer brewed by G. Ovens, its proprietor.
Arriving at the bar, he found his old friend James Piper
there, and was saddened to see that he looked as gloomy
as ever.

Sir James had been a disappointment to Gally ever
since the latter's return to Blandings Castle. He had not
expected to find the sprightly young Jimmy Piper of the
old Pelican days, for he knew that long years in Parliament, always having to associate with the sort of freaks
who get into Parliament nowadays, take their toll; but he
had anticipated a reasonable cheerfulness, and such was
Jimmy's moroseness that it could not be explained merely
by the circumstance of his having perpetually on the
back of his neck a sister like Brenda. After all, Gally felt,
he himself had ten sisters, four of them just as bad as
Brenda, but you never heard unmanly complaints from
him.

Gally was not a man to beat about bushes. He welcomed
this opportunity of solving a mystery which had been
annoying him, and embarked on his probe without
preamble.

'What on earth's the matter with you, Jimmy? And
don't say "Nothing" or talk a lot of guff about the cares of

office weighing on you. A man doesn't necessarily go about looking like a dead fish because he's Home Secretary, or whatever you are. I've known Home Secretaries who were as cheerful as stand-up comics. No, something is biting you, and I want to know what it is. Confide in me, Jimmy, bearing in mind that there was a time when our minds were open books to each other. You've given me enough material to write your biography, only I suppose it wouldn't do now that you are such a big pot. Still, let's have the latest instalments.'

It was only for a moment that Sir James hesitated. Then, for G. Ovens's home-brew has above all other beverages the power to break down reticences, he said:

'Can I confide in you, Gally?'

'Of course.'

'I badly need advice.'

'I have it on tap.'

'You remember in the old days how crazy I was about your sister Diana?'

'I remember.'

'I still am. You'd think I would have got over it, but no. The moment I saw her again, it was just as bad as ever.'

His statement was one which might have seemed sensational to some auditors, but Gally took it calmly. He had the advantage of having given up many hours of his valuable time to listening to a younger James Piper expressing himself on the subject of the woman he loved; and if he was surprised, it was only because he found it remarkable that the fire of those days should still be ablaze after all those years.

That his sister Diana should be the object of this passion occasioned him no astonishment. He had always placed her in the top ten for looks, charm and general *espièglerie* and had shared in the universal consternation when she had thrown herself away on an ass like Rollo Phipps.

44

'Good for you, Jimmy,' he said. 'If you are trying to find out if I approve, have no anxiety. When the wedding ceremony takes place, you can count on me to be in the ringside pew lending a fairly musical baritone to The Voice That Breathed o'er Eden or whatever hymn you may have selected. Now that Diana has been so satisfactorily de-Phippsed I could wish her no better husband.'

Sir James had imbibed a full tankard of G. Ovens's home-brew and was halfway through his second, and that amount of the elixir is generally calculated to raise the spirits of the saddest into the upper brackets, but the cloud remained on his brow, darker than ever.

'The wedding ceremony isn't going to take place,' he said bitterly.

Gally leaped to the obvious conclusion, and his eye glass, as if in sympathy, leaped to the end of its string.

'Don't tell me you've changed your mind.'

'Of course not.'

'Then why this pessimistic outlook? Did she turn you down?'

'I haven't proposed.'

'Why not?'

'I didn't get the chance.'

'I thought you were going to say you discovered you had some incurable disease and had been given two weeks to live, which would of course have spoiled the honeymoon. The trouble with you politicians,' said Gally, 'is that you wrap up your statements to such an extent with double-talk that the lay mind needs an electric drill to get at the meaning. Tell me in a few simple words what the hell you're talking about.'

'I can tell you in one. Murchison.'

'Who's Murchison?'

'My bodyguard.'

'Have you a bodyguard?'

'Sergeant E. B. Murchison. A Chancellor of the

Exchequer has to have a bodyguard, assigned to him by Scotland Yard.'

Gally shook his head.

'You ought never to have let them make you Chancellor of the Exchequer, Jimmy. If I had known, I would have warned you against it. What does this fellow Murchison do? Follow you around?'

'Wherever I go.'

'You must feel like Mary with her lamb, though I doubt if anyone attached to Scotland Yard has fleece as white as snow. I begin to see now. Your style is necessarily cramped. If you pressed your suit and Diana proved co-operative, your immediate impulse would be to fold her in a close embrace, and you wouldn't want a goggling detective looking on.'

'Exactly. I'm a shy man.'

'Are you?'

'Very shy.'

'That makes it worse. I've never been shy myself, but I can understand how you feel. No chance of you stiffening the sinews, summoning up the blood and having a pop at it regardless of Murchison?'

'None.'

'Then we must think of something else.'

'I have thought of something else. I'm going to write her a letter.'

'Outlining your sentiments?'

'Yes.'

Gally was not encouraging.

'Dismiss the idea. A letter is never any good, especially if it's from someone like you, most of whose adult life has been spent in politics. You've got so accustomed to exercising caution and not committing yourself that you simply aren't capable of the sort of communication which hits a woman like a sock in the solar plexus and makes her say to herself, "Lord love a duck, this boy's got what it

46

takes. I must weigh this proposal of his carefully or I'll be passing up the snip of a lifetime".'

James Piper finished his home-brew and heaved a sigh.

'You make it all seem very hopeless, Gally.'

'Nothing is hopeless, if you have a Galahad Threepwood working for you,' said Gally. 'I have solved problems worse than yours in my time, so buck up and let us see that merry smile of yours that goes with such a bang in the House of Commons.'

CHAPTER SEVEN

THERE were times, it seemed to Gally some days after his heart to heart talk with James Piper at the Emsworth Arms, when the grounds and messuages of Blandings Castle came as near to resembling an enchanted fairyland as dammit. Strong hands had mowed the lawn till it gleamed in the sunlight, birds sang in the tree tops, bees buzzed in the flower beds. You would not be far wrong, he thought, if you said that all Nature smiled, as he himself was doing. His mood was mellow, its mellowness increased by the fact that, slipping adroitly from the table at the conclusion of lunch, he had secured the hammock under the cedar before the slower Florence could get at it. She came out of the house just after he had moved in, and it set the seal on his euphoria to note her thwarted look, comparable to that of baffled baronets in melodramas he had seen at the Lyceum and other theatres in his younger days. It was the keystone of his policy always, if possible, to show his sisters, with the exception, of course, of Diana, that they weren't everybody.

His strategy was effective. Florence took her book elsewhere. But he knew it was too much to expect that his siesta would remain undisturbed indefinitely. Nor did it. Scarcely had his eyes closed and his breathing become deeper, when a respectful finger poked him in the ribs and he woke to see Beach at his side.

'Mr. Galahad,' said Beach.

'Ah, Beach, Beach,' he replied, 'I was having a lovely dream about backing a long shot for the Grand National and seeing it come in by a length and a half. Are you here just to have a chat?'

'No, sir,' said Beach, shocked. He would chat freely with Mr. Galahad in the seclusion of his pantry, but not on the front lawn. 'A Mr. Smith has called, asking to see you.'

For an instant the name conveyed nothing to Gally. Then memory stirred, and he sat up with enthusiasm.

'Bring him along, Beach,' he said. 'Nobody you know, but he's just the fellow I hoped would be calling,' and he was on his feet and prepared to welcome Jeff when Beach produced him, which he did some moments later with what amounted to a flourish. Any friend of Mr. Galahad got the V.I.P. treatment from Beach. He then melted away as softly and gracefully as was within the power of a butler who would never see fourteen stone again, and Gally and Jeff were, as the former would have put it, alone and unobserved.

'My dear boy,' said Gally, 'this is splendid. I was half afraid you would lose your nerve and not come.'

'Nothing would have kept me away.'

'You Smiths do not know what fear is?'

'Only by hearsay. Nice place you have here.'

'We like it. But there is a catch. I don't know if you are familiar with the hymn about spicy breezes blowing o'er Ceylon's isle?'

'Where every prospect pleases and only man is vile.'

'Exactly. However, it's the women you have to watch out for, rather than the men. If you had a classical education, you will remember the Gorgon who used to turn people to blocks of ice[25] with a glance. My sister Florence, whom you will be meeting in a moment, is like that when offended.'

'I can see the solution there. I won't offend her.'

'You have already done so. You have come to paint the Empress's portrait, to be added to those in the family portrait gallery, and she is as sick as mud about it. When she is as sick as mud about anything she stiffens from the soles of her feet upwards and gives the offending party the sort of look the Gorgon used to give people. Being her brother and exposed to it from childhood, I am immune to this, but I always warn strangers to be sure to make their wills before getting together with her, just in case. Some people will tell you that she isn't as bad as my sister Connie. How right Kipling was when he made that crack about the female of the species being more deadly than the male. Look at our family. My brother Clarence is as gentle a soul as ever said "What ho!" to a pig, and I, as you must have noticed already, am absolutely charming, but the only one of my sisters whom I would not be afraid to meet down a dark alley is Diana.'

It would be idle to deny that these grave words gave young Mr. Smith a disagreeable sinking sensation in the neighbourhood of the third waistcoat button, but love conquers all, as someone once said, and he thought of Vicky and was strong again. He might be about to be turned into a block of ice, but the weather was warm and he would eventually thaw out again and see Vicky once more. He told Gally that his plans were unaltered, and Gally said it did him credit.

'The great thing to bear in mind,' said Gally, 'is that sisters are sent into the world to try us and make us more spiritual. I attribute my own spirituality entirely to having been brought up in the same nursery as Connie and Hermione and Dora. It taught me fortitude and a sense of proportion. When I went out into the great world, I met a variety of tough eggs, but always I was able to say to myself "Courage, Galahad, this egg is unquestionably hard to cope with, but he isn't Connie or Hermione or Dora!" You wouldn't believe the things that went on in that nursery. My sister Hermione once laid me out cold with one blow of her doll Belinda. Am I scaring you?'

'Yes,' said Jeff.

'You quail at the thought of meeting Florence?'

'Yes,' said Jeff.

'But you are prepared to go through it?'

'Yes,' said Jeff.

'Good. Let us hope that this will be one of her good mornings,' said Gally, and he took him to Beach and told Beach to take him to Lady Florence, which Beach did, and Gally returned to his hammock.[26]

Before he could reach it he met Sir James Piper coming across the lawn and was pained to see his careworn aspect. Sir James was looking as an investor in some[27] company might have looked on learning that its managing director had left England without stopping to pack.

'Stap my vitals, Jimmy,' said Gally, 'you look like the Mona Lisa.[28] You remind me of the last time I saw you chucked out of the old Gardenia. The same wan expression as the hand of the Law closed on coat collar and trouser seat. What's wrong? Or needn't I ask?'

'You needn't.'

'The same little trouble you were having when we chatted at the Emsworth Arms?'

'Yes.'

'I'll give you a pep talk.'

'I haven't time for any pep talks. I'm playing croquet[29] with Diana. She's waiting for me now.'

It is always pleasant for a man of good will to be given the chance of bringing the roses back to the cheeks of a stricken friend, and Gally lost no time in availing himself of this one.

'Croquet!' he cried. 'Then, my dear fellow, what on earth are you making heavy weather about? Don't you know that there is no surer way to a woman's heart than that footling game? At least there usedn't to be when I was ass enough to swing a mallet in my youth. In those days eighty per cent of betrothals took place on the

51

croquet lawn. The opportunities for whispering words of
love into shell-like ears are endless. If I hadn't been sent
to South Africa, where they didn't play, I should have
been engaged half a dozen times before I was twenty-five.
So buck up, Jimmy. Go ahead and fear nothing. I see you
bringing off a sensational triumph.'

'With Murchison looking on?'

Gally's enthusiasm waned perceptibly.

'I'd forgotten Murchison,' he said.

'I hadn't,' said Sir James. 'I never do.'

It was shortly after he had passed on to keep his tryst,
with E. B. Murchison following in his footsteps like King
Wenceslaus's page, that Gally, back in the hammock and
thinking happily how comfortable Florence would have
been if she had got there first, was roused from his
musings by the arrival of Vicky.

Vicky was looking bewildered, as if strange things had
been happening around her which she felt that only
Gally with his greater wisdom could explain. Though she
was not hopeful that even Gally would be able to find an
explanation for what was weighing on her mind at the
moment except the unwelcome one that that mind was
tottering.

'Gally,' she said, 'do you think you can see things that
aren't there?'

'Do you mean ghosts? Clarence's pig man claims to
have seen the White Lady of Blandings one Saturday
night as he was coming out of the Emsworth Arms at
closing time. One cannot, however, dismiss the theory
that he was pie-eyed at the time. Why do you ask?'

'Because I've just seen Jeff.'

'Ah, yes.'

'Is that all you can say?'

'You were bound to see him some time, now that he's
here.'

'He's *here*?'

'Yes, I got him the job of painting the Empress.'

Vicky uttered what in a girl less attractive would have been a squeal. She was conscious of a weakness about the knees. Her grandmother in similar circumstances would have swooned.

'Gally,' she said, 'I think I'm going to collapse on you.'

'Come along. Plenty of room.'

'Or shall I just gaze at you with adoring eyes?'

'Whichever you prefer. When you meet him, by the way, you must remember to address him as Mister Smith. He is here strictly incognito.'

'I'll remember.'

'Well, mind you do.'

'Don't be afraid I'll let the side down. I've read lots of secret service stories and I know the procedure. I will now,' said Vicky, 'gaze at you with adoring eyes.'

She was proceeding to do so, when a figure, well-knit though inclining to stoutness, appeared on the lawn. Sir James Piper, closely followed by Sergeant E. B. Murchison.

'Hullo,' said Gally as his old friend reached the hammock. 'Finished your croquet already?'

Sir James hastened to dispel any idea he may have had that that leisured pastime had been affected by the modern craze for speed.

'We haven't begun yet.'

'What's the trouble?'

'Daphne wanted her large hat.'

'I don't wonder. The sun is very sultry and we must avoid its ultry-violet rays, as the song says.[30] Well, I won't keep you. Don't forget what I told you.'

'What did you tell him?' Vicky asked as Sir James resumed his quest for large hats.

'To push croquet to its logical conclusion.'

'Whatever that means.'

'I will explain when it's cooler.'

'Explain now.'

'It's quite simple. He's in love with your Aunt Diana, and I was pointing out to him . . . Ah, here he is, complete with hat. You've got that Mona Lisa look again, Jimmy. What's wrong?'

'Nothing's exactly wrong, but I wish Brenda would mind her own business. She's sent my secretary down here in case, she says, I need him.'

'Well, don't you? I would have thought he was the very chap you would want to have around if any weighty thoughts occurred to you. You'd look pretty silly if an idea for balancing the budget occurred to you and you forgot it because there was nobody to take it down in his notebook.'

'I'm supposed to be on holiday.'

'You mustn't think so much of holidays, Jimmy. Life is stern and earnest. You ought to be floating loans or whatever it is you do in your job, and a secretary is essential. However, as you seem determined to live for pleasure alone, I will leave you to your croquet.'

'The last thing I want is Claude Duff following me about with his note book. It's bad enough having Murchison. But two of them!'

Words failed Sir James and he passed on, and Gally was so moved that he sat up in the hammock and dropped his eyeglass.

'Claude Duff!' he exclaimed. 'Oh my fur and whiskers!'

'What's the matter?'

'Ruin stares us in the eyeball.'

'Because Claude Duff is here?'

'Exactly.'

'Why?'

'Because,' said Gally, 'he is an intimate friend of your Jeff and will undoubtedly call him by his real name in front of Florence the moment they meet.'

CHAPTER EIGHT

THE SUN was shining as brightly as ever, the birds and bees respectively singing and buzzing with undiminished vigour, but Vicky did not notice them. Her whole attention was monopolized by her Uncle Galahad, who had turned misty and was flickering like an old-time silent picture.

'Oh, Gally,' she wailed. 'Oh, Gally!'

He had no comfort to offer. It was with a sombre look on his face that he retrieved the eyeglass which was dancing on the end of its string.

'You may well say "Oh, Gally",' he said. 'I wouldn't blame you if you made it something stronger.'

'This is frightful!'

'The situation has certainly started to deteriorate.'

'He'll be thrown out.'

'On his ear. "Chuck this man as far as he'll go, and I want to see him bounce twice", Florence will say to the hired help. Unless I have an inspiration.'

'Oh, do try.'

'I am trying, and I think I'm getting the glimmering of an idea. But I shall need a few minutes' solitude if I am to develop it. I can't possibly plot and plan with you having conniption fits at my elbow. Leave me, child, I would be alone. Trot off and pick flowers.'

'How long?'

'Short stalks.'

'I mean how long do you want to be alone?'

'Call it a quarter of an hour.'

'Will that be enough?'

'It should be.'

'You're wonderful, Gally.'

'I always was from my earliest years. It's a gift.'

Vicky was one of those girls who are anxious to help. She gave Gally twenty minutes instead of the quarter of an hour he had specified. When she returned to the hammock, she found him so obviously pleased with himself that it was unnecessary to ask questions. She thrilled with relief and for the first time was able to appreciate the efforts of the sun, the birds and the bees, which all this while had been giving of their best.

'I've got it,' said Gally. 'The solution turned out to be a very simple one. I shall see Claude before he meets Jeff and I shall tell him the tale.'

'You'll do what?'

'Tell him the tale.'

'I don't follow you, Mr. Threepwood.'

'You don't know what is meant by telling the tale?'

'No.'

'Then in order to explain I shall have to take you back to my impecunious youth, when I combined a taste for wagering on horses with an inability to spot which of the contestants was going to finish first. In a word I was one of the mugs and in constant debt to turf accountants who liked one to settle one's obligations with the minimum of delay. Fortunately I was born with the gift of persuasive eloquence. Mug though I was, I could tell a tale. When at my best, I could make bookies cry and sometimes lend me a fiver to be going along with.'

'What used you to say to them?'

'It wasn't so much what I said as the tone of voice. I had the same knack Sarah Bernhardt had of tearing the heart strings.'

'I hope you were ashamed of yourself.'

'Oh, bitterly.'

'You must have been a very disreputable young man.'

'So I was often told by my nearest and dearest. I was one of those men my mother always warned me against.'

'Well, it's lucky you're such a low character. A saintly uncle wouldn't have been much use in the present crisis. I suppose, when you tell the tale, you deviate from the truth a lot?'

'Quite a good deal. I have always found the truth an excellent thing to deviate from.'

'What are you going to say to Mr. Duff?'

'Hullo, Duff. Nice to see you again. Lovely weather, is it not. I shall then give him the works.'

'I can hardly wait.'

'You won't have to, for here he comes, no doubt to report to Jimmy on the croquet lawn.'

This was indeed Claude's purpose, for in addition to being nervous he was conscientious and never shirked his duty, even when unpleasant. His employer, sometimes inclined to be irritable, always gave him the same uneasy feeling as affected him when meeting strange dogs, but he faced him bravely and hoped for the best.

It was, however, without enjoyment that he was going to meet him now, and the sight of Gally, who at their previous encounter had proved so genial a companion, cheered him greatly. So when Gally said 'Hullo, Duff. Nice to see you again. Lovely weather, is it not?' his response was the cordial response of one confident of having found a friend.

'This is Miss Underwood, my niece,' said Gally.

'How do you do?' said Claude.

'How do you do?' said Vicky.

There was a pause. Claude tried to think of a bright remark, but was unable to find one. He regretted this, for Vicky had made a profound impression on him. He substituted a not very bright question.

'Did you find Jeff all right?'

57

'I did indeed.'

'Good old Jeff. I wish I saw more of him.'

'You will. And I should like a word with you before you meet him.'

'Meet him?'

'He's here.'

'What, at the castle?'

'That very spot.'

'That's certainly a surprise. Is he here for long?'

'He won't be if the powers of darkness hear you calling him Jeff.[31] His true identity must be wrapped in a veil of secrecy. Smith is the name to which he answers.'

'I don't understand.'

'I am about to brief you. This incognito stuff is to avoid him being given the bum's rush by my brother Clarence.'

'I still don't . . .'

'You will in a minute. Are you familiar with the facts about Jeff's father?'

'No. What about his father?'

'I shall be coming to that in a moment, but first let me get quite clear as to the relations between you and Jeff. Did I gather correctly from what you were saying when we met at Eastbourne that you and he had been at school together?'

'That's right. Wrykyn.'

'A most respectable establishment.'

'We were in the same house. Our last two years we shared a study.'

'So you were constantly in happy comradeship, now brewing tea and toasting sausages, anon out on the football field, rallying the forwards in the big game.'

'I wasn't in the football team. Jeff was.'

'Or sitting side by side in the school chapel, listening to the chaplain's short manly sermon. What I'm driving at is that, linked by a thousand memories of the dear old school, you wouldn't dream of saying or doing anything to give Jeff a jab in the eye with a burned stick, thus causing him alarm and despondency and rendering his hopes and dreams null and void.'

Claude could not quite follow all the ramifications of this, but he grasped the general import and replied that he could be relied on not to do anything damaging to Jeff's hopes and dreams.

'Good,' said Gally, 'then we can proceed. He is after the job of secretary[32] to my brother Clarence, and his position is a bit tricky. I don't know if you had any difficulty in getting taken on in a similar capacity by Jimmy Piper?'

'No, there wasn't any trouble. My father worked it. He's pretty influential, and he's a great friend of Sir James.'

'How different from Jeff's father. He's dead now, but in his lifetime he was a dishonest financier who ruined hundreds before skipping the country. He did my brother Clarence down for several thousands of the best and brightest, and Clarence is very bitter about it. Clarence, I must tell you, is a man of ungovernable passions, and did he discover that Jeff was the son of the man who got into his ribs for that substantial sum, there would be no question of engaging him as his secretary. He would probably bite him in the leg or throw an ormolu clock or something at him. His fury would be indescribable. That is why I beg you to remember on no account to call Jeff Jeff in his presence. Smith is the name. You understand?'

'Oh, rather.'

'Splendid. What a treat it is dealing with a man of your lightning intelligence. You don't know what a relief it is to feel that we can rely on you. Remember. Not Jeff. Smith. Though as you are such old friends you might call him Smithy.'

'At school we always called him Bingo.'

59

'That will be capital. Well, I am glad it's all straightened out, my dear Duff. You had now better be getting along and reporting to Jimmy. No doubt he will be delighted to see you.'

Vicky had been listening to these exchanges with growing admiration. As Claude receded in the direction of the croquet lawn, she said:

'At-a-boy, Gally.'

'Thank you, my dear.'

'I see now what you mean by telling the tale.'

'I was not at my best, I fear. One gets a bit rusty as the years go by. Still, it got over all right.'

'Triumphantly.'

'We shan't have any more trouble with Claude Duff. So now there's nothing on our minds.'

'Nothing.'

'We are carefree. We sing tra la la.'

'Would you go as far as that?'

'Omitting perhaps the final la!'

'Though I shall be too nervous to do much singing.'

'Nonsense. Nothing to be nervous about.'

'You really feel that?'

'Certainly. I don't say that when Jimmy told us Claude Duff had clocked in I didn't feel a momentary twinge of uneasiness. But you saw how soon it passed off. What can possibly bung a spanner into our hopes and dreams now? It isn't as if your stepmother was your Aunt Constance. Connie could detect rannygazoo by a sort of sixth sense and smell a rat when all other noses were baffled, but she was a woman in a thousand. Sherlock Holmes could have taken her correspondence course.'

'What a comfort you are, Gally.'

'So I have been told, though not by any of the female members of my family. What a lot of exercise Beach is taking this afternoon,' said Gally, changing the subject as the butler came out of the house and made his way towards them. 'Hullo, Beach. Did you want to see me, or are you out for a country ramble?'

Neither of these suggestions, it appeared, fitted the facts. It was duty that had called Beach to brave the ultra-violet rays of the sun.

'I am taking his lordship a telegram that has just come over the telephone. It is from Mr. Frederick, saying that he is in England again and will be paying a visit to the castle as soon as his business interests permit.'

Beach passed on, and Vicky, starting to express her pleasure at the prospect of seeing her Cousin Frederick again, found herself interrupted by a sharp barking sound from her Uncle Galahad, who, becoming coherent, added the words 'Hell's bells!'

'What's the matter?' she asked.

Gally was in no mood to break things gently.

'Do you realize,' he said, his voice choked and his eyeglass once more adrift, 'that we are plunged more deeply in the soup than ever? Freddie is a friend of Jeff's and you know what a bubblehead Freddie is. The chances that he won't call Jeff Jeff in front of your stepmother are virtually nil.'

'Oh, Gally.'

'There is only one thing to do—go to London and intercept him and make him see that he must not come down here. I'll pinch the Bentley[33] and start right away.'

CHAPTER NINE

JEFF meanwhile, conducted by Beach, had come to journey's end, but he was under no illusion that his pilgrimage was to terminate in lovers' meeting. His emotions on finding himself closeted with Florence somewhat resembled those of a young lion tamer who, entering the lion's cage, suddenly realizes that he has forgotten all he was taught by his correspondence school. A chill seemed to have fallen on the summer day, and he saw how right Gally had been in comparing his sister to the late Gorgon.

Forbidding was the adjective a stylist like Gustave Flaubert would have applied to her aspect, putting it of course in French, as was his habit. She was an angular woman, and her bearing was so erect that one wondered why she did not fall over backwards. She had not actually swallowed some rigid object such as a poker, but she gave the impression of having done so, and Jeff was conscious of surprise that she should have succeeded in getting married to one so notoriously popular with the other sex as J. B. Underwood.[34] Perhaps, he felt, he had proposed to her because somebody betted he wouldn't.

Beach, having announced 'Mr. Smith' in a voice from which he did his best to keep the gentle pity he could not but feel for the nice young man he was leaving to face her ladyship in what was plainly one of her moods, withdrew, and Florence opened the conversation.

Some women who at first sight intimidate the beholder set him at his ease with charm of manner. Florence was not one of these. Her 'How do you do', delivered from between clenched teeth, was in keeping with her appearance, and Jeff's morale, already in the low brackets, slipped still lower. No trace remained of the airy confidence with which he had assured Gally that the Smiths knew what fear was only by hearsay. A worm confronted by a Plymouth Rock would have been more nonchalant.

Florence came to the point without preamble.

'I understand that you have come to paint a portrait of Lord Emsworth's pig,' she said, speaking as if the words soiled her lips.

'Yes,' said Jeff, only just checking himself from adding 'ma'am'. It was difficult not to believe himself in the presence of Royalty.

'It is a perfectly preposterous idea.'

There seemed nothing to say in reply to this, so Jeff said nothing. Nobody knew better than himself that he was getting the loser's end of these exchanges, but there seemed nothing he could do about it. He envied Gally, who, he knew, would have taken this haughty woman in his stride.

'Pigs!' said Florence, making it clear that these animals did not stand high in her estimation, and while Jeff was continuing to say nothing the door opened and Lord Emsworth pottered in with his customary air of being a somnambulist looking for a dropped collar stud.

'Florence,' he bleated, 'I've just had a telegram from Frederick. He says he's in England again and is coming here.'

There was no pleasure in his voice. Visits from his younger son seldom pleased him. Freddie was a vice-president of Donaldson's Dog Joy of Long Island City, N.Y. and like all vice-presidents was inclined to talk shop. It is trying for a father who wants to talk about nothing but pigs to have a son in the home who wants to talk about nothing but dog-biscuits.

63

'Oh?' said Florence.

'I thought you would like to know.'

'I haven't the slightest interest in Frederick's movements.'

'Then you ought to have.'

'Why?'

'You're his aunt.'

If Florence had been less carefully brought up, she would no doubt have said 'So what?' As it was, she chose her words more carefully.

'I am not aware that there is a law, human or divine, which says that an aunt must enjoy the society of a nephew who confines his conversation exclusively to the subject of dog-biscuits.'

'*Noblesse oblige*,' said Lord Emsworth, remembering a good one, and Florence asked him what on earth *noblesse* had got to do with it. As Lord Emsworth was unable to find a reply to this, there was a momentary silence, during which Jeff decided that if there was going to be an argument about what was and what was not required behaviour for aunts, it was a good time to leave. He sidled out, and Lord Emsworth, seeing him for the first time, gazed after him in bewilderment, almost as if, like his pig man, he had been suddenly confronted by the White Lady of Blandings, who was supposed to make her rounds of the castle with her head under her arm, it having been chopped off by her husband in the Middle Ages.

'Who was that?' he asked, and Florence was obliged to soil her lips again.

'Mr. Smith,' she said.

'Oh, yes. He's come to paint the Empress.'

'So I understand.'

'He's a friend of Galahad's.'

'I do not consider that a great recommendation.'

'Nice young fellow I thought he looked.'

'He struck me as a criminal type. He's probably known to the police.'

'I don't think so. Galahad said nothing about him being friends of theirs. Odd his disappearing like that. I must find him and take him to see the Empress.'

'Are you really serious about putting that pig's portrait in the portrait gallery?'

'Of course I am.'

'You will be the laughing-stock of the county.'

Gally would have replied that a good laugh never hurt anybody, but Lord Emsworth was more tactful.

'I don't know why you say that. There will be a plaque, don't you call them, at the side of the picture about her being three years in succession silver medallist in the Fat Pigs class at the Shropshire Agricultural Show, an unheard-of feat. People will be too impressed to laugh.'

'A pig among your ancestors!'

'Galahad says she will lend the gallery a tone. He says that at present it is like the Chamber of Horrors at Madame Tussaud's.'

'Don't talk to me about Galahad. The mere mention of his name upsets me.'

'I thought you were having one of your spells. You get them because you're so energetic all the time. You ought to lie in the hammock in the afternoons with a book. Well, I can't stay talking to you all day, I must be going and finding Smith,' said Lord Emsworth.

Jeff was in the corridor, warming up after his session with the Snow Queen. Lord Emsworth greeted him briskly. Already, brief though their acquaintance was, he had taken a great fancy to Jeff.

'Ah, there you are, Mr. Smith. I am sorry my sister was having one of her spells when you arrived. She always has them when she starts thinking about putting the Empress's portrait in the portrait gallery. It does something to her. It was the same with my sister Constance, now in America married to an American whose name I have forgotten. She, too, always had these spells when the matter of the Empress's portrait came up. But you will be wanting to see her. Not Constance, the Empress. It is quite a short distance to her sty.'

He led Jeff through the kitchen garden and into a meadow dappled with buttercups and daisies, making pleasant conversation the while.

'Things,' he said, 'have settled down now that the Empress has retired and no longer competes in the Shropshire Agricultural Show, but when she was an active contestant one was never free from anxiety. There was a man living in a house near here who kept entering his pigs for the Fat Pigs event and was wholly without scruples. One always feared that he would kidnap the Empress or do her some mischief which would snatch victory from her grasp. He was a Baronet. Sir Gregory Parsloe.'

Here he paused impressively, seeming to suggest that Jeff must know what baronets were like, and Jeff agreed that they wanted watching, and they reached the sty in perfect harmony.

The Empress was having an in-between-meals snack, her invariable practice when not sleeping, and Jeff regarded her with awe.

'I've never seen such a pig,' he said.

'Nobody has ever seen such a pig,' said Lord Emsworth.

'Good appetite.'

'Excellent. You can't imagine the bran mash she consumes daily.'

'Well, nothing like keeping body and soul together.'

'You would think that anyone would be proud to paint her. And yet all these Royal Acadamecians refused.'

'Incredible.'

'In fact, my dear fellow, you are my last hope. If you fail me. I shall have to give up the whole thing.'

'I won't fail you,' said Jeff.

He spoke sincerely. The affection Lord Emsworth felt for him was mutual. Say what you might of the ninth Earl—his limpness, the way his trousers bagged at the knees and the superfluity of holes in his shooting jacket— he was essentially a lovable character and Jeff was resolved to do all that was within his power to make him happy. And if the Gorgon objected and had spells, let her have spells.

CHAPTER TEN

GALLY had no difficulty in finding Freddie. A man in London on an expense account generally tends to do himself well, and Freddie, when sent across the Atlantic by his father-in-law to promote the interests of the English branch of Donaldson's Dog Joy, never watched the pennies. It was in a suite at the Ritz that the meeting between uncle and nephew took place. Freddie was having a late breakfast.

Gally was surprised to see a cloud on his nephew's brow, for normally Freddie was a cheerful young man, inclined perhaps, as his Aunt Florence had said, to confine his talk to the subject of dog-biscuits, but uniformly cheerful. His sunny smile, Gally had always understood, was one of the sights of Long Island City, but now it no longer split his face. It was with a moody fork that he pronged the kippered herring on his plate, and not even James Piper could have more closely resembled the Mona Lisa as he sipped coffee.

Gally noted these symptoms with interest. His experienced eye told him that they were not due to a hangover, so it would seem that some business worry was causing this depression.

'Something on your mind, I see,' he said. 'Is it that trade is not brisk?'

'Trade is a pain in the neck,' said Freddie, abandoning the kipper and going on to marmalade. 'In England I mean, not in America. I have not a word of criticism of the American dog, whose appetite for biscuits remains the same as always. But the dogs over here . . . Old Donaldson will have a fit when I turn in my report.'

Gally's face took on a grave expression in keeping with the solemnity of the moment, but he had come here on a mission of vital importance and was not to be diverted from the main issue.

'I'm sorry,' he said, 'but before going into that in depth I will explain why I wanted to see you. Your cousin Victoria—'

'I don't know what England's coming to.'

'Your cousin Victoria has fallen in love with the wrong man and is immured at Blandings, and I have got the man there under a false name. I can reveal this to you without reserve as you have been associated with me in many of my cases. You will recall the Bill Lister incident.'[35]

'And I'll tell you why trade isn't brisk,' said Freddie. 'It's because of the bad practice of English dog owners of giving their dogs scraps at the luncheon and dinner tables. I was lunching—'

'Freddie—'

'I was lunching at a house in Sussex only yesterday, and there was my hostess with a dog on each side of her, and all through the meal she kept giving them hand-outs, yes, even of the Bavarian Cream which was the final course.'

'Freddie—'

'Is it reasonable to suppose that a dog full of Bavarian Cream will be satisfied with a biscuit, even one as wholesome and rich in all the essential vitamins as Donaldson's Dog Joy? Naturally when I produced a sample and offered it to the animals they backed away, turning up their noses, and I was unable to book an order. And the same thing has happened over and over—'

'Freddie,' said Gally, 'if you don't stop babbling about your damned dog-biscuits and listen to me, I'll shove the remains of that kipper down your neck.'

Freddie looked up from his marmalade, surprised.

'Were you saying something?'

'I was trying to. It's about Jeff Bennison.'

'I know Jeff Bennison.'

'I know you do.'

'What about him?'

'He and Vicky are in love.'

'Nothing wrong with that, is there?'

'Yes, there is, because Florence has imprisoned her at Blandings to get her out of Jeff's way and I have got Jeff into the house, calling himself Smith.'

'You mean he's in?'

'Yes, he's in.'

'Hob-nobbing daily with Vicky?'

'Yes.'

'Absolutely on the premises?'

'Yes.'

'Then what's your problem?'

'I wouldn't have one if you hadn't wired Clarence that you were coming to Blandings . . . You mustn't come within a hundred miles of the place. Go anywhere else in England that takes your fancy—they say Skegness is very bracing—but keep away from Shropshire.'

'I don't get it. Why?'

'Because the first thing you would do when you got there would be to say—in Florence's presence—"Bless my soul if it isn't my old friend Jeff Bennison. How are you, Jeff old man, how *are* you?" '

Freddie was offended. Had he not been seated, he would undoubtedly have drawn himself up to his full height.

'Are you insinuating that I am a beans-spiller?'

'Yes, I am.'

'I've been given medals for keeping things under my hat.'

'You didn't get one in the Bill Lister affair. I got Bill into the castle incognito in order to oblige my niece Prudence, they being deeply enamoured and kept apart by various relatives. You probably remember the affair . . .'

'Of course I do, and let me tell you—'

'So what occurred? We were all having tea as cosy as be blowed, when you burst in through the french window and bellowed "Blister! Well, well, well! Well, well, well, well, well! This is fine, this is splendid! I can't tell you how glad I am, Prue, that everything is hunky-dory". Then, addressing Prue's mother, you said that Prue could find no worthier mate than good old Bill Lister, where-upon, as might have been foreseen, she had him out of the house in three seconds flat. We don't want that sort of thing happening again.'

If Freddie had not finished his marmalade, he would have choked on it, so great was his indignation.

'Well, dash it,' he thundered, 'I don't see how you can blame me. It stands to reason that if a chap has been established as a pariah and an outcast and you suddenly find him tucking into tea and buttered toast in company with the girl's mother, you naturally assume that the red light has turned to green.'

'Yes, I can see your side of it,' said Gally pacifically. It was no part of his policy to rouse the fiend that slept in Freddie's bosom. 'But I still think it would be safer if you didn't come to Blandings.'

Freddie was all cold dignity.

'I have no wish to come to Blandings,' he said. 'I was only going there to give the guv'nor a treat. He enjoys my visits so much.'

'Then that's settled,' said Gally, relieved. 'A pity, of course, that you won't see Jeff.'

'As a matter of fact,' said Freddie, 'I'm not particularly anxious to see Jeff. He gave me a comic strip thing to sell in America, and I couldn't land it anywhere, and I'm afraid he'll be thinking I've let him down.'

CHAPTER ELEVEN

BY inciting the Bentley to make a special effort Gally was enabled to reach Blandings Castle just in time to dress for dinner. It was not till he joined the company at the table that he became aware that unfortunate things must have been happening in his absence. If the atmosphere was not funereal, he told himself, he did not know a funereal atmosphere when he saw one, and it perplexed him. For moodiness on the part of James Piper he had been prepared, and he had not expected anything rollicking from his sister Florence, but Jeff and Vicky should surely have been more vivacious. Their gloom was as marked as that of Freddie had been when brooding on the mistaken liberablity of the English dog owner. Vicky was pale and cold, and Jeff crumbled a good deal of bread.

At the conclusion of the meal there was a general move to the drawing-room, but Jeff went out on to the terrace, and Gally followed him there, eager for an explanation. When a man has gone all the way from Shropshire to London to further the interests of a young protégé, he resents it when the latter shows no appreciation of his efforts. It was with an offended rasp in his voice that he opened the conversation.

'Jeff,' he said, 'you look like the seven years of Famine we read of in Scripture. You could go on and play King Lear without make-up. Before going into the reasons for this — possibly you have been having another spell in the frigidaire with Florence — let me tell you a bit of news which ought to bring the sun smiling through. I saw Freddie, and I have headed him off.'

'You've done what?'

Gally could make nothing of the question. It bewildered him.

'Didn't Vicky tell you he was planning to come here?'

A spasm of pain contorted Jeff's face as if he were discovering too late that he had swallowed a bad oyster. His voice, when he replied, trembled.

'Vicky isn't speaking to me.'

'What do you mean, she isn't speaking to you? Got tonsilitis or something?'

'We've quarrelled.'

It was the last thing Gally was expecting, and he felt as a general might feel if his whole plan of campaign had been ruined by some eccentricity on the part of his troops. He had taken it for granted that, whatever else might go wrong, the love of his two clients could be relied on to remain unchanged.

'Quarrelled?' he gasped.

'Yes.'

'One of those lovers' tiffs?'

'Rather more than that, I'm afraid.'

'Big-time stuff?'

'Yes.'

'Your fault, of course?'

'I suppose so. She wanted me to elope with her, and I wouldn't.'

'Why not?'

'Because it would have meant letting Lord Emsworth down. He told me himself I was his last hope of getting the Empress painted. And another thing. What on earth would we have lived on? Unless Freddie sells that strip of mine. Did he say anything about that, by the way?'

Gally was grateful for the question. He had been wondering how to break the bad news.

'I'm afraid he did, my boy.'

That word 'afraid' could have only one meaning. Jeff

gave a momentary quiver, and his mouth tightened, but he spoke calmly.

'Nothing doing?'

'Nothing.'

'About what I expected. It was very good of Freddie to bother himself with the job.'

His courageous bearing under the shattering blow increased Gally's already favourable opinion of Jeff. At Jeff's age he, like all Pelicans, had accepted impecuniosity as the natural way of life. If you had the stuff, you spent it; if you hadn't, you borrowed it. He had sometimes been best man at weddings where the proceedings were held up while the groom, short by fourteen shillings of the sum required of him, fumbled feverishly in his pockets, his only comment 'Well, this is a nice bit of box fruit, if you like.'

But Jeff, he knew, was different from the young Galahad. Jeff took life seriously. And very proper, too, the reformed Galahad felt.

'The future doesn't look rosy,' he said.

'Not excessively,' said Jeff.

'It's the old story — where's the money coming from?'

'That's it in a nutshell.'

'Isn't there anything you can do?'

'I'm a pretty good architect, but what good is that when I can't get commissions?'

'True. But first things first. We can't have you at outs with Vicky. I shall now proceed to sweeten her.'

'Fine, if you can do it. How do you propose to?'

'I shall tell her the tale,' said Gally.

Vicky was at the piano in the smaller drawing-room, playing old English folk songs, as girls will when their love life has gone awry. Gally's face was stern and his eye austere as he approached her. He was not pleased with her behaviour. Life, he considered, was difficult enough without girls giving excellent young men the pink slip and going off and playing old English folk songs.

'I've just been talking to Jeff,' he said, wasting no time with polite preliminaries. 'And don't sit there playing the piano at me,' he added, for this was what Vicky was continuing to do. 'He tells me you won't speak to him. Nice goings-on, I must say. He comes here, braving all the perils of Blandings Castle to be with you, and you give him the push. I can't follow your mental processes. Of course the fact of the matter is that you would now give anything if you could recall those cruel words.'

'What cruel words?'

'You know damn well what cruel words.'

'Must we discuss this?'

'It's what I came here to do.'

'You're wasting your time.'

'Oh, don't be a little idiot.'

'Thank you,' said Vicky, and she played a few bars of an old English folk song in a marked manner.

It occurred to Gally that he was allowing exasperation to interfere with his technique. Instead of telling the tale he was letting this tête-à-tête degenerate into a vulgar brawl. He hastened to repair his blunder.

'I'm sorry I called you an idiot.'

'Don't mention it.'

'I was not myself.'

'Who were you?'

Sticky going, Gally felt, extremely sticky going. The tale he told would have to be a good one. And fortunately his brain, working well, had come up with a pippin.

'The fact is,' he said, ignoring the question, which would not have been easy to answer, 'this unfortunate affair has woken old memories. There was a similar tragedy in my own life. Two loving hearts sundered owing to a foolish quarrel, and nothing to be done about it because we were both too proud to make the first move. It happened when I was a very young man and sadly lacking in sense. I loved a girl. I won't tell you her name. I will call her Deirdre.'

'I've often wondered how that name was spelled,' said Vicky meditatively. 'I suppose you start off with a capital D and then just trust to luck. Was she beautiful?'

'Beautiful indeed. Lovely chestnut hair, a superb figure and large melting eyes, in colour half way between a rook's egg and a bill stamp.[36] I loved her passionately, and it was my dearest wish to call her mine. But it was not to be.'

'Why wasn't it?'

'Because of my unfortunate sense of humour. She was the daughter of a bishop, very strict in her views.'

'And you told her one of your Pelican Club limericks?'

'No, not that. But I took her to dinner at a fashionable restaurant and thinking to amuse her I marched round the table with a soup plate on my head and a stick of celery in my hand, giving what I thought was a droll impersonation of a trooper of the Blues on guard at Whitehall. It was a little thing I had often done on Saturday nights at the Pelican to great applause, but she was deeply offended.'

'She thought you were blotto?'

'She did. And she swept out and married an underwriter at Lloyd's. I could have explained, but I was too proud.'

'Her cruel words had been too cruel?'

'Exactly.'

'How very sad.'

'I thought you would think so.'

'Though it would be a lot sadder if you hadn't told me that Dolly Henderson was the only woman you had ever wanted to marry. Deirdre must have slipped your memory.'

It was not easy to disconcert Gally. Not only his sisters Constance, Hermione and Florence, but dozens of book-

makers, policemen, three-card men and jellied eel
sellers had tried to do it through the years and failed, but
these simple words of Vicky's succeeded in doing so. As
he stood polishing his eyeglass, for once in his life unable
to speak, she continued her remarks.

'You certainly have nerve, Gally. The idea of trying to
tell *me* the tale. One smiles.'

Gally was resilient. Not for him the shamefaced blush a
the sheepish twiddling of the fingers. Recovering quickly
from what had been an unpleasant shock, he spoke in a
voice very different from his former melting tones.

'Oh, one does, does one?' he said. 'Well, one won't smile
long. Listen to me, and I'm not telling the tale now. Jeff
refused to sit in on your chuckleheaded idea of eloping for
a very good reason.'

'He said he had to stay on and paint a pig.'

'That wasn't his only reason. He also didn't want to
have to see you starving in the gutter. He had no job and
no prospects and he knew that you had a good appetite
and needed three squares a day.'[37]

'How absolutely absurd. I've all sorts of money.'

'Held in trust for you by your stepmother.'

'She'd have given it to me.'

'Want to bet?'

'Anyway we'd have got along somehow. There are a
hundred things Jeff could have done.'

'Name three. I can only think of two—robbing a bank
and stealing the Crown Jewels. The trouble with you,
young Victoria, is that you're like all girls, you don't look
ahead. You want something, and you go for it like a
monkey after a banana. The more prudent male counts
the cost.'

'When have you ever counted the cost?'

'Not often, I admit. But I'm not a prudent male. Jeff's
different.'

There was a pause. Gally's voice had lacked the Sarah

Bernhardt note which had come into it when he had been telling the tale, but his words, even without that added attraction, were such as to give food for thought, and they had made Vicky look pensive. She played a bar or two with an abstracted air.

'I've thought of something,' she said suddenly.

'That's good. What?'

'There wouldn't be any need for us to starve in gutters. Freddie will sell that thing of Jeff's at any moment and we'll be all right even if I can't get my money. They pay millions for these comic strips in America, and they go on for ever. And when you're tired of doing the work yourself you hand it over to someone else and get paid just the same. Look at some of them. About as old as Blandings Castle, and I'll bet the fellows who started them have been dead for centuries.'

Gally saw that the time had come to acquaint this optimistic girl with the facts of life.

'I was about to touch on the J. Bennison comic strip,' he said. 'Don't expect a large annual income from it. Freddie tells me he has tried every possible market and nobody wants it. However promising an architect Jeff may have been, he apparently isn't good at comic strips. Don't blame him. Many illustrious artists would have had the same trouble. Michelangelo, Tintoretto and Holbein are names that spring to the mind.'

Gally's prediction that it would not be long before his niece ceased to smile was fulfilled with a promptitude which should have gratified him. If a bomb had exploded in the smaller drawing-room, scattering old English folk songs left and right, she could not have reacted more instantaneously. The haughtiness which had been so distasteful to her uncle fell from her like a garment.

'Oh, Gally!' she cried, her voice breaking and her attractive eyes widening to their fullest extent. 'Oh, the poor darling angel, he must be feeling *awful.*'

'He is,' said Gally, holding the view that this softer mood should be encouraged. 'His reception of the news was pitiful to see. It knocked him flatter than a Dover sole. He reminded me of Blinky Bender, an old pal of mine at the Pelican, the time when he won sixty pounds on the fourth at Newmarket and suddenly realized that in order to collect the money he would have to go past five other bookies in whose debt he was. You had better run along and console him.'

'I will.'

'Making it clear that all is forgiven and forgotten and that you are sweethearts still,' said Gally, and he went off to get a glass of port in Beach's pantry.

CHAPTER TWELVE

JEFF had gone to his room after dinner and changed into a sweater and flannel trousers. There was a full moon, and it was his intention to sit on the terrace in its rays.[38] Not that he expected anything curative to come of this. He did not share Gally's confidence that telling the tale to Vicky would pick up the pieces of a shattered world and glue them together as good as new. He was aware that in his time Gally with his silver eloquence had played on hardened turf commissioners as on so many stringed instruments, but he could not but feel that the gifted man was faced now with a task beyond even his great powers. Those cruel words to which Gally had alluded in his conversation with Vicky were still green in Jeff's memory, and it was difficult to imagine a tale, however in the Sarah Bernhardt manner it might be told, persuading their speaker to consider them unsaid.

A knock on the door interrupted his sombre meditations, the diffident knock of one not sure of his welcome, and Lord Emsworth entered looking like a refugee from a three-alarm fire. He had removed the dress clothes which his sister Florence compelled him to don for dinner and put on the familiar baggy trousers and tattered shooting coat which few tramps would not have been too fastidious to appear in in public.

'Ah, Mr. Smith,' he said, 'I hope I am not disturbing you.'

Jeff, though solitude was above all what he desired at the moment, assured him that he was not, and Lord Emsworth wandered to and fro, picking things up and dropping them, his habit when in a room new to him.

'I thought you might like to come and see the Empress by moonlight,' he said in the manner of someone inviting a friend to take a look at the Taj Mahal.

Six simultaneous things he would have preferred to do flashed through Jeff's mind, but consideration for a host of whom he had become very fond kept him from mentioning them and he replied that that would just make his day.

'But will she be up?' he asked, and Lord Emsworth asked up where.

'Won't she have gone to bed?'

'Oh, no, she always has a snack at about this hour.'

'Bran mash?'

'That and the other things prescribed by Wolff-Lehmann. According to Wolff-Lehmann, whose advice I follow to the letter, a pig to be in health must consume daily nourishment amounting to fifty-seven thousand eight hundred calories, these to consist of proteins four pounds seven ounces, carbohydrates twenty-five pounds.'

'It doesn't leave her much time for anything else.'

'No, she has few other interests.'

'Nothing like sticking to what you do best.'

'Exactly. We will go out by the back door and through the kitchen garden. It is the shortest way.'

The route indicated took them past Beach's pantry, and they could hear the butler's fruity laugh, indicating that Gally was telling him some humorous story from his deplorable youth. It surprised Jeff that anyone could laugh in the world as at present constituted. He himself was sunk in a gloom on which not even the prospect of seeing Empress of Blandings by moonlight could make an impression.

Lord Emsworth, on the other hand, was bright and chatty. He had returned to the subject of Sir Gregory Parsloe, on which he knew that his young friend would wish to be fully informed. It was not far to the Empress's sty, and the Parsloe saga provided absorbing, if one-sided conversation all the way. If Jeff had had any doubts as to the depths of infamy to which baronets could sink,[39] they were resolved by the time he reached his destination. He did not suppose he would ever meet Sir Gregory Parsloe, but if he did he told himself he would be careful not to buy a used car from him.

At the sty Lord Emsworth paused.

'Have you a flask with you?' he asked.

'I beg your pardon?'

'A flask of whisky.'

This surprised Jeff. He had not suspected his host of being a drinking man, and in any case it seemed to him that the other might have quenched his thirst before leaving the house. He said he was sorry but he had not, and Lord Emsworth looked relieved.

'I asked because on one occasion somebody drank from a flask while at the rails of the sty and dropped it into the Empress's trough,[40] and I am sorry to say that she became completely intoxicated. My brother Galahad, I remember, suggested that she ought to join Alcoholics Anonymous, and I was very doubtful whether the committee would accept a pig. Fortunately we discovered the truth. But it was an anxious time.'

'It just shows you,' said Jeff.

'It does indeed,' said Lord Emsworth.

The Empress, as predicted, was having a late snack, and for what seemed to Jeff several hours they stood gazing at her. Eventually she appeared to feel that she had had sufficient to see her through till breakfast and retired to the covered portion of the sty, there to curl up and get the wholesome slumber which Wolfe-Lehmann no doubt considered essential to her health. Reluctantly Lord Emsworth led the way back to the house, and Jeff was privileged to hear how Sir Gregory Parsloe, stopping at nothing, had decoyed George Cyril Wellbeloved, Lord Emsworth's superbly gifted pig man, from service at the castle to his own employment.

Entering through the back door, they separated, Lord Emsworth to proceed to his room and read Whiffle's *On the Care of the Pig*[41] for an hour or so before going to bed, Jeff to fulfil his original intention of sitting on the terrace in the moonlight.

It was soon after this that Gally bade Beach good night and Beach, having heard Lord Emsworth come in and remembering how often after these night expeditions he forgot to lock up, went to inspect the back door.

It was as he had thought. The door was not locked.

He locked it.

Jeff, meanwhile, thankful to be alone, though naturally sorry that he was to hear no more about Sir Gregory Parsloe, continued to sit in the moonlight, smoking his pipe and looking on the dark side of things.

Jeff was one of those rare young men whose hearts once bestowed, are bestowed for ever. In a world filled to overflowing with male butterflies flitting and sipping and then moving on to flit and sip somewhere else he remained as steadfast as Jacob or any of the others who became famous for their constancy. He had fallen in love with Vicky at their first meeting and he had been in love with her ever since, and the fact that he was now so low in her estimation made no difference to him. He had friends who in the same position, deprived of the girl they loved, would have consoled themselves with the thought that there would be another one along in a minute, but this easy philosophy was not for J. G. Bennison. The current situation made J. G. Bennison feel that hope was dead.

How long he would have sat there had nothing occurred to divert his thoughts, he could not have said, but one of the charms of the English climate is its ability to change from high summer to midwinter in a matter of minutes, and a bitter wind springing up from the east persuaded him that he would be more comfortable in bed.

It is rather saddening to think that his first emotion on reaching the back door and finding it locked was a surge of anti-Lord Emsworth feeling, for there was nothing to indicate that that absentminded peer was not responsible for the devastating act. Nothing could be truer to form than that his host should have locked up, completely forgetting that he had left a companion out on the terrace. Showing once again that in human affairs it is always the wrong man who gets the blame. Beach, who should have played the stellar role in Jeff's commination service, escaped without a curse.

Two courses were open to Jeff. He could ring bells and hammer on doors till he roused the house or he could stay outside for the night. Neither appealed to him. It was improbable that the first alternative would bring Lady Florence down in a dressing gown, but it was a possibility, and the thought of being pierced by those icy eyes was one that intimidated even a Smith who knew what fear was only by hearsay. On the other hand, with the wind freshening, remaining in the great outdoors offered few attractions.

It was as he stood there, this way and that dividing the swift mind, as somebody once put it, that he had a vague recollection, when on the terrace, of having seen an open window not very far above him, a window well within the reach of one who in his undergraduate days at Oxford had mastered the knack of climbing up walls and sliding through windows after lock-up. He had wondered whose it was.

Externally Blandings Castle might have been specially designed for the climber's convenience. Stout strands of ivy had been allowed to flourish on its walls till the merest novice would have experienced no difficulty in finding his way up.

A minute later he was window bound, glad to find that the old skill had not deserted him. Five minutes later he was across the sill. And twenty-five seconds after that the quiet night was disturbed by a noise like the shattering of a hundred dishes falling from the hands of a hundred waiters, and he was staggering across the floor with a bruised shin and drenched trouser legs. The occupant of the room, as he was to discover later, had placed beneath the window a jug full of water, several assorted fire irons, a chair, a picture of sheep in a meadow and another picture of a small girl nursing a kitten.

Lights flashed on, and a voice spoke, the voice of Claude Duff.

'Stick 'em up, or I shoot,' it said. 'It's all right shooting a burglar,' it added. 'I asked my solicitor.'[42]

CHAPTER THIRTEEN

THAT JEFF, climbing through the window in the dark, should have become entangled in fire irons, jugs of water and pictures of sheep and kittens was not surprising, for these had been stacked in close ranks, impossible to avoid. It was also less than extraordinary that he should have felt irritated with Claude Duff. A drier and less bruised man might have applauded Claude's prudence in consulting his solicitor before starting to take human life. Jeff felt only annoyance, and he expressed this in his opening words, which were:

'Oh, don't be a damned fool.'

'Jeff!' cried Claude in ringing tones, and Jeff snarled a reminder that danger lurked in addressing him thus. Who knew that Lady Florence was not even now with her hand on the door handle, all ready to join their little circle? The fire irons alone had made enough noise to wake a dozen Florences.

'I thought you were a burglar,' said Claude.

'Well, I'm not.'

'What *are* you exactly?' Claude asked. 'I mean, climbing up walls and sliding through windows. Conduct surely a bit on the eccentric side. No son of mine would do that sort of thing unless he were rehearsing for pantomime.'

'I was locked out by old Emsworth,' Jeff replied, though he should have said 'old Beach'. 'He took me out to see his pig by moonlight, and he forgot that I had gone on to the terrace. Tell me,' he went on more amiably, for the agony of his shin was now abating, 'What were those things doing on the floor?'

There was modest pride in Claude's voice as he answered the question.

'That was my own unaided idea. I can't sleep without a window open, so I always open one and set a booby-trap in case of burglars. I'm glad you turned out not to be one, for between you and me I was stretching the facts a bit when I said I was going to shoot. I haven't a gun.'

'But all right otherwise?'

'No complaints at all. I like it here. The slight crumpled rose leaf is that Piper's sister will be arriving at any moment. She's a terror.'

'She can't be worse than Florrie.'

'My dear chap, she begins where the latter leaves off. Not that Lady Florence is a woman you would care to meet late at night down a dark alley. I was amazed when I thought she was Vicky's mother. Great relief when I found she was only step.'

'Vicky!'

The word had shot from Jeff's lips like a projectile.

'She asked me to call her Vicky.'

Jeff could not speak. He had not seen Claude Duff for some time, but he knew all about his uncanny gift for ensnaring the female heart. Women fell before him like ninepins and he was always falling before women. Not once but on several occasions Jeff had had to listen to outpourings from him reminiscent of the Song of Solomon. And Vicky, her eyes opened to the defects of J. G. Bennison, would be quite likely to fall under his spell, if she had not fallen already. Jeff had lost her, no argument about that, but that did not debar him from being shocked, horrified, appalled and rendered speechless by the prospect of her becoming another's.

Claude took advantage of his dumbness to proceed.

'I wouldn't say this to anyone except you, Jeff, but I'm in love. I've thought I was several times, I know, but this is the real thing. She was with Mr. Threepwood when I arrived yesterday, and he introduced us. "This is my niece Miss Underwood," he said, and in a flash something told me I had met my ideal. It was the way she looked. You've probably not noticed, but she has a sort of sad expression, as if she had had some great sorrow in her life. One longs to pick her up and kiss her and comfort her. Do you believe in love at first sight, Jeff?'

Long association with Claude had given Jeff plenty of opportunity of making up his mind about this phenomenon, even if he had not had his own experience to guide him, but still unable to speak, he answered neither in the affirmative or the negative, and Claude continued.

'It's an odd thing that this should have happened, because up till now I've always been attracted by tallish girls, and Vicky's so small and dainty. What are those statuette things you hear people talking about? Tan something.'

Jeff was apparently unable to help him, for he remained silent.

'Tan?' said Claude, snapping his fingers. 'Tan? Tan? Tanagra,' he said, inspired. 'She's a Tanagra statuette. I've never seen one, but I know what they must be like. Jeff, old man, do you think I have a chance. She's not engaged to anybody, is she?'

'No,' said Jeff, speaking for the first time. It was a point on which he was well informed.

'Then I may have a chance. Do you think I have a chance, Jeff? We got along like a couple of sailors on shore leave, and fortunately money is no problem. A secretary doesn't make a fortune, though I hope you'll stick old Emsworth for a packet when and if, but I can lay my hands on something better any time I want to. One of my uncles is Duff of Duff and Trotter, and he's always after me to go into the business. I've held off so far because of the prestige of being with Piper, but now that I plan to get married . . .'

Jeff could bear no more.

'Good night,' he said.
'But, Jeff, don't go yet, old man.'
'Good *night*,' said Jeff.

It was with heart bowed down that he sought the seclusion of his bedroom. He had supposed it already bowed down about as far as it could go, but he realized now that he had underestimated its capabilities for sinking. There is a difference, subtle but well-marked, between the emotions of a lover who has been told by the girl he loves that all is over between them and those of a lover who, tottering from this blow, sees a Claude Duff beginning to exercise his fascinations on her. In the former case he has a hope, if only a weak one; in the latter, merely despair.

Jeff was a modest man and could think clearly, and he was miserably conscious that between himself and a charmer like Claude Duff there could be no contest. Take looks, for instance. They ought not to count, but they do. And he was what dramatic critics call adequate. Claude was spectacular.

Claude could play the piano, always a gift of maximum assistance to a wooer. And in addition to this he had only to fall in with his uncle's wishes to have plenty of money at his disposal. It was ridiculous to hope to compete with a man so armed at every point.

With Jeff so sunk in the slough of despond it might have seemed that nothing could bring him even momentarily to the surface; but that this feat could be accomplished was proved before he had gone the length of the corridor. All that was needed was for someone to steal up behind him, tap him on the shoulder and say 'Ho'. Sergeant Murchison, appearing from nowhere, did this, and Jeff came out of his thoughts with a start which could not have been more violent if, like Lord Emsworth's pig man, he had seen the White Lady of Blandings.

CHAPTER FOURTEEN

THE TROUBLE about being the chronicler of a place like Blandings Castle, where someone is always up to something and those who are not up to something are up to something else, is that you have so many people to write about that you tend to push quite deserving characters into the background. Sergeant Murchison is a case in point. Mention, it is true, has been made of him from time to time, but only casual mention. Not a word has been said of the way he felt about things, not a syllable concerning his love for Marilyn Poole, Lady Diana's maid, and the public is left without a clue as to whether he liked his daily duties or disliked them.

Now it can be told. His daily duties gave him the heeby-jeebies. In jaundiced mood he regarded himself as a bird in a gilded cage. It was as distasteful to him to have to follow Sir James Piper wherever he went as it was to Sir James to be followed. Often he thought wistfully of the brave old days when he had been a simple constable walking a beat in Whitechapel or Bottleton East with platoons of drunks and disorderlies on every side, inviting him to make a pinch. Where, he asked himself bitterly, were those pinches now? Gone with the wind, one with Nineveh and Tyre.

It can be readily appreciated, therefore, that when, smoking at his window and thinking of Marilyn and her distressing habit of flirting with Sir James's chauffeur, he saw a sinister figure climbing up the castle wall, he had felt as the poet Wordsworth used to do when he beheld a rainbow in the sky. (Wordsworth's heart, it will be remembered, always leaped up when this happened.) To race downstairs would have been with him the work of an instant if he had not slowed himself up by tripping over a loose mat.

However, the marauder was still there when he reached the corridor, so he crept up behind him, tapped him on the shoulder and said 'Ho'.

The effect of this on Jeff was electrical. To have hands tapping him on the shoulder and voices saying 'Ho' where no hands or voices should have been would have startled the most phlegmatic man. He rose perhaps six inches into the air and came to earth too short of breath to speak. Sergeant Murchison took it on himself to keep the conversation going.

'You're pinched,' he said.

'Pinched!' said Jeff, recovering enough breath for the simple monosyllable.

'Pinched,' said Sergeant Murchison, and would have spelled the word if so desired.

This completed Jeff's illusion of having lost his reason. Oh, what a noble mind is here o'erthrown, he might have said to himself if he had remembered the quotation. All he could find to say was a feeble 'How do you mean pinched?' and Sergeant Murchison said he meant pinched.

'Who are you?' Jeff asked. It is always well to know the identity of the officer pinching us.

'Sergeant E. B. Murchison, special representative of Scotland Yard. And I'm taking you to Lord Emsworth, who will decide what's to be done with you.'

And so it came about that Lord Emsworth, deep in Whiffle's *On the Care of the Pig*, was wrenched from its magic pages by the entry of two intruders, one young Smith, whom he had come to love as a son, the other someone he did not remember having seen before. However, any friend of his friend Smith was a friend of his, and he liked the affectionate way the man was holding on to Smith's arm, so he welcomed the pair warmly.

'Come in, my dear Smith, come in Mr. er, er. I'm sorry, I keep forgetting your name. You know how one does.'

'Murchison, m'lord.'

'Of course. Murchison. Quite.'

'Of Scotland Yard.'

This puzzled Lord Emsworth.

'But that's in London, isn't it?'

'Yes, m'lord.'

'Then what are you doing in Shropshire?'

Jeff was able to answer this.

'He's arresting me.'

'Doing what?'

'Arresting me.'

'Why?'

'For making a burglarious entry,' said Sergeant Murchison.

Something stirred in Lord Emsworth. His memory might be poor where recent events were concerned, but it was excellent about things that had happened thirty years ago, especially if these were of no importance whatsoever.

'Bless my soul,' he said, 'that reminds me of a song in a musical comedy Galahad took me to when we were young men. About the Grenadier Guards guarding the Bank of England at night. How did it go? "If you've money or plate in the bank," sang Lord Emsworth in a reedy tenor like an escape of gas, "we're the principal parties to thank. Our regiment sends you a squad that defends you from anarchists greedy and lank." '

'M'lord,' said Sergeant Murchison.

' "In the cellars and over the roof," ' continued Lord Emsworth, who was not an easy man to stop, ' "we keep all intruders aloof, and no-one can go in to rob Mr. Bowen of what he describes as the oof." Bowen must have been the manager of the Bank of England at that time, don't you think?'

'M'lord,' said Sergeant Murchison.

' "That's our right. And if any wicked gentry try by night to make a burglarious entry, they take fright at the sight of the busbied sentry." '[43]

'M'lord,' said Sergeant Murchison, 'this man was climbing up the castle wall and getting in at one of the windows.'

'I was locked out,' said Jeff.

'Very sensible of you to climb up the wall, then.'

'I didn't like to rouse the house.'

'Very considerate of you. Different from Baxter, a former secretary of mine. He was locked out one night and he threw flower pots in at my window. A most unpleasant experience to be asleep in bed and have the air suddenly become thick with flower pots.[44] A flower pot can give you a nasty bruise. But how, my dear Mr. Murchison,' said Lord Emsworth, reasoning closely, 'can Smith have been making a burglarious entry when he's staying here?'

'He's staying here?' Scotland Yard trains its sons well. They remain unmoved under the worst of shocks. Sergeant Murchison had seldom received a more disintegrating blow, but he did not so much as totter 'You know him?'

'He is the artist who is painting the portrait of my pig.'

Sergeant Murchison was a man who could face facts. He did not need further evidence to tell him that the pinch of which he had thought so highly had been but a mirage. He turned and left the room.

'I don't much like your friend Murchison,' said Lord Emsworth, as the door closed. 'He reminds me of my sister Constance. The same look on his face, as if he suspected everybody he met. Constance is now in America. You are not American, are you?'

'No.'

'I thought you might be. So many people are nowadays. Constance married an American. I went out there for the wedding. Do you know that in America they give you boiled eggs mashed up in a glass?'

'Really?'

'I assure you. It takes away all the fun of eating a boiled egg. A most interesting country, though. Galahad used to go there a great deal at one time. Galahad was always the adventurous type. Peanut butter.'

'I beg your pardon?'

'It is much eaten in America. I was told that you put jam on it. If you like jam, of course. And after they have finished eating peanut butter they go out and contact people and have conferences. Which reminds me. That step-daughter of my sister Florence's, I forget her name but you have probably met her, nice girl, she often gives the Empress a potato, she is trying to contact you. I met her roaming about the place and she asked me if I had seen you, because it was most important that you and she should have a conference. You're not leaving me, are you, my dear fellow?'

Jeff was leaving him. He was already at the door. Hope, so recently consigned to the obituary column, had cast off its winding cloths and risen from the grave. Lord Emsworth might see nothing sensational in the fact that Vicky was roaming about the place trying to confer with him, but to Jeff it was so significant that the world suddenly became a thing of joy and laughter and even Lord Emsworth in his old shooting coat and baggy trousers seemed almost beautiful.

Girls, he knew, changed their minds. They thought things over and reversed decisions. The girl who on Monday hissed that she never wanted to see you again was quite likely to be all smiles and affection on Tuesday —or at the latest at some early hour on Wednesday.

It came, accordingly, as no surprise to him when he met Vicky not far from Lord Emsworth's door and she flung herself into his arms with the words 'Oh, Jeff, darling!' They stood locked together, the past forgotten, and Lord Emsworth, coming out of his room, eyed them with paternal benevolence.

Lord Emsworth had come out of his room because he hoped that Jeff was still within reach. He wanted to discuss with him the question, which they had omitted to touch on, of whether Jeff should depict the Empress full face or in profile. He refrained from bringing this up at a moment when the young fellow's mind was so obviously on other things, so he went back into his room and sat there for some time plunged in thought.

The result of his thoughts was to send him to the room of his sister Florence.

'Oh, Florence,' he said, 'could I have a word with you?'

'I hope it is important, Clarence. I was asleep.'

'It is. Very important. Do you remember coming to me some time ago and kicking up no end of a row because your step-daughter was in love with a fellow named Bennison?'

'I remember mentioning it,' said Florence with dignity. She disliked his choice of phrases.

'Well, you can make your mind easy. She isn't in love with Bennison at all. The chap she loves is my friend Smith. I saw them just now hugging and kissing like the dickens.'

CHAPTER FIFTEEN

FLORENCE may have been asleep at the moment when Lord Emsworth knocked on her door, but she was wide awake now. It was her practice to put mud on her face before retiring to rest, and such was her emotion as he delivered what a gossip column writer would have called his exclusive that this mud cracked from side to side like the mirror of Tennyson's Lady of Shalott.

'Is this a joke, Clarence?' she demanded, directing at him a look lower in temperature even than those which Jeff had had to face on his arrival. 'Are you trying to be funny?'

'Certainly not,' said Lord Emsworth indignantly. He had not tried to be funny since the remote days of school, when it had taken the form of pulling a chair away from a friend who was about to sit down. 'I tell you I saw them. I came out of my room and there they were, as close together as the paper on the wall. I was delighted, of course.'

'Delighted?'

'Naturally. I knew how greatly you objected to the chap you thought Victoria was in love with, and what could be better than that she should have had second thoughts while there was still time and taken up with my friend Smith, a charming fellow thoroughly sound on pigs?'

'And a penniless artist who has to take any tuppenny job that's offered to him.'

'If you consider painting the portrait of Empress of

Blandings a tuppenny job, I disagree with you,' said Lord
Emsworth with dignity. 'And he isn't a penniless artist.
Galahad tells me he is very well off, and only paints pigs
because he loves them.'

At the sound of that name Florence started so violently
that more mud fell from her face. Experience had taught
her that no good could ever come of anything with which
Galahad was connected. She began to feel like the man in
the poem who on a lonely road did walk in fear and dread
and having once looked back walked on and turned no
more his head, because he knew a frightful fiend did close
behind him tread. Galahad and frightful fiends, not much
to choose between them. She was normally a pale woman,
as any woman with a brother like that had a right to be,
but now she turned scarlet.

'Galahad!' she cried.

'Smith's a friend of his. It was he who arranged for him
to come to the castle. I had been trying with no success to
get Royal Academicians and people like that to paint the
Empress, but Galahad said No, what I wanted was an
eager young enthusiastic chap like Smith. So he sounded
him about coming here, and fortunately he was at
liberty. So he came. But I mustn't keep you up. You're
anxious to turn in. Is that mud you've got on your face?
How very peculiar. I always say you never know what
women will be up to next. Well, good night, Florence,
good night,' said Lord Emsworth, and he trotted off to
renew his interrupted study of Whiffle.

If he had supposed that on his departure Florence
would curl up and go to sleep, he erred. Late though the
hour was, nothing was further from her thoughts than
slumber. She sat in a chair, her powerful brain working
like a dynamo.

It was of Galahad that she was thinking. It seemed
incredible that even he could have had the audacity to
introduce into Blandings Castle the infamous Bennison at

the thought of whom she had been shuddering for weeks, but he might well have done so. Long association with him had told her that the slogan that ruled his life was Anything Goes.

CHAPTER SIXTEEN

BRENDA PIPER, one of those hardy women who do not mind getting up early, caught the 8.30 express to Market Blandings[45] on the following morning, and Jno Robinson took her to the castle in his taxi.

The last time Jno and his taxi appeared in this chronicle was when he had Gally as a passenger and then, it will be remembered, there was a complete fusion of soul between employer and employed and the most delightful harmony prevailed. It was very different on this occasion. Briefness of acquaintance never deterred Brenda from becoming personal and speaking her mind. If in her opinion someone she had only just met required criticism, criticism was what he got.

Jno Robinson had not yet shaved. She mentioned this. His costume was informal, of the Lord Emsworth school rather than that of Beau Brummell. This too, was touched on. She also thought poorly of his skill as a driver, and said so. The result was that when they drew up at the front door of Blandings Castle it needed only the discovery that she did not approve of tipping to round out the ruin of Jno Robinson's day.

Before going in search of her brother James, Brenda presented herself to her hostess and was concerned to see how pale she was. Florence, as has been indicated, had slept badly.

'Good gracious,' she exclaimed. 'What ever is the matter, Florence? Are you ill? If it's a cold coming on, take two aspirins and go to bed.'

Florence shook her head. It was not medical advice she needed.

'I had a bad night, but I'm perfectly well. It's Victoria. You know the trouble I am having with her. That man of hers.'

'Surely not now that she is at the castle?'

'But he is here, too.'

'*Here?*'

'Galahad sneaked him in. Clarence wanted someone to paint his pig, and Galahad produced this man.'

'You're sure he's the one?'

'Quite sure.'

'Then —'

'Why don't I turn him out? Because I have no proof. You know how often you hear that the police are certain that somebody has done some crime, but they cannot make an arrest until they have proof. It's the same here.'

'I'd kick him out and chance it.'

'It would mean trouble with Clarence. Of course if I had proof there would be no difficulty. Even Clarence could not object then.'

Privately Brenda did not attach much importance to any possible objections on Lord Emsworth's part, but she abstained from her customary candour because she was thinking. The trend of her thoughts became evident a moment later.

'I know what you can do,' she said. 'Didn't you tell me that Victoria told you that this man Bennison had been employed as a drawing instructor at Daphne Winkworth's school? Well, ring up Daphne and get a description of him.'

'I'll do it at once,' said Florence. She felt that one could always rely on Brenda.

She hastened to the telephone.

'Daphne.'

'Who is this?'

'Florence.'

'Oh, how are you, Florence dear?'

'Very worried. I rang up to ask you to do something for me.'

'Anything, of course.'

'It's just to describe a man named Bennison.'

'Do you mean who used to be here as drawing master?'

'Used to be! Aha!'

'Why do you say Aha?'

'Because I suspect Galahad of having sneaked him into Blandings under a false name.'

'Galahad is capable of anything.'

'Anything.'

'I won't enquire as to his motives. Being Galahad – one can assume that they were bad . . .'

'They were.'

'Well, Mr. Bennison is about five foot eleven, well built, clean shaven, fair hair, and he has a small scar just under his right eye. A football accident, I believe. I wouldn't say for certain that his nose hadn't been broken at some time. Does this meet your requirements?'

'It does,' said Florence. 'It does indeed. Thank you, Daphne. I am very grateful to you.'

Armed with this information, she went out into the grounds in search of Gally. She found him in the hammock under the cedar and for once took no offence at his occupancy of it. A sister about to bathe a brother in confusion and, though she could not count on this, bring the blush of shame to his cheek, has no time to bother about hammocks.

She was all amiability as she opened her attack.

'Having a little sleep, Galahad?'

'Not at the moment. Thinking deep thoughts'

'About what?'

'Oh, this and that.'

'Cabbages and kings?'

'That sort of thing.'

'Did you meditate at all on Mr. Smith?'

'Not that I remember.'

'I thought you might have been wondering why he called himself that.'

'Why shouldn't he? It's his name.'

'Really? I always thought his name was Bennison.'

Gally's training at the old Pelican Club stood him in good stead. Membership at that raffish institution always equipped a man with the ability to remain outwardly calm under the impact of nasty surprises. Somebody like Fruity Biffen, taken aback when his Assyrian beard fell off, might register momentary dismay, but most members beneath the slings and arrows of outrageous fortune were able to preserve the easy nonchalance of a Red Indian at the stake. Gally did so now. Nobody could have told that he was feeling as though a charge of trinitrotoluol had been touched off under him. His frank open face showed merely the bewilderment of a brother who was at a loss to know what his sister was talking about.

'Why on earth should you think his name was Bennison?'

'Because last night Clarence saw him hugging and kissing Victoria. It seemed to me odd behaviour if they had only known each other about twenty-four hours.'

Gally was astounded.

'He was kissing her?'

'Yes.'

'You accept Clarence's unsupported word?'

'Yes.'

'You don't think he was having one of those hallucinations people have?'

'I do not.'

'I knew a chap at the Pelican who thought he was being followed about by a little man with a black beard. Well, I will certainly speak to Smith about this. But I still think Clarence must have been mistaken.'

'Have you known him long?'

'Ages. We grew up together.'

'You did what?'

'Oh, you mean Smith. I thought you meant Clarence. Yes, I've known Smith quite a while. Not so long as I've known Clarence, of course, but long enough to be sure he's just the man Vicky ought to marry.'

'And I'm sure that his name is Bennison and that you brought him to the castle.'

Gally shook his head reproachfully. He was not angry, but you could see he was terribly hurt.

'You ought not to say such things, Florence. You have wounded me deeply.'

'Good.'

'You have caused me great pain.'

'You'll distribute it.'

'What beats me is where you got this preposterous notion.'

'I ought to have told you that. From my friend Daphne Winkworth, at whose school Mr. Bennison was employed for quite a time. She gave me a most accurate description of him, down to the scar you will have noticed under his right eye. Well, I think that is all, Galahad, and you may go back to your deep thinking. I have of course told Victoria that Mr. Bennison is leaving the castle immediately.'

WORK IN PROGRESS

YOU HAVE just read the last chronicle of Blandings: sixteen skeleton chapters of a Wodehouse novel that was to have gone to twenty-two.

These sixteen chapters, typed out on Wodehouse's favourite old 1927 Royal and their pages numbered 1–90, were in the hospital with him when he died on February 14th 1975. In addition, one hundred and eighty-three pages of notes and drafts for this novel were found after his death, thirty-three of them in the hospital, one hundred and fifty of them from among the papers in his study at home. Practically all of these pages were in his own handwriting, but only eighteen of them were date-lined on top. Usually Wodehouse date-lined every page, not only of his self-communing notes in preparation of a novel's scenario, but also of his drafts of dialogue and narrative.

Among the pages of notes he had with him in hospital were two, obviously consecutive, in typescript, of which the first is dated January 19th 1975. Although these two pages indicate that Chapter 16, which you have just read, was typed out after that date, the January 19th pages carry the last date that Wodehouse put on any page of the collection. And, if you want to know how the last six chapters might have brought the novel to a happy ending, this January 19th scenario (pages 150–155) is the key document.

You will see that, at this stage, Wodehouse

1. is proposing to give his hero, Jeff, a less reprobate father. The father will now be Beach the butler's brother, and an actor rather than an absconding company director.

But it is not clear from the scenario why Beach is 'agitated' about this. Is it because he thinks that Lady Florence will oppose the Jeff/Vicky romance even more strongly if she discovers that Jeff, in addition to being penniless and an impostor, is also nephew to the castle's butler?

2. has not decided what to do about Florence's husband. After some doubts (page 161) he is clearly going to *be* her husband, and somehow their separation has to be changed to reconciliation and bright hopes of happiness together in the future;

3. has left Claude Duff in the air and unattached;

4. has not decided how Jeff is going to assure himself of an income sufficient to enable him honourably to marry the soon-to-be-rich Vicky. If other objections (see 1 above) are overcome, Florence might believe Gally's enthusiastic assurances about Jeff's future in Chapter 22, at least for long enough to loosen the purse-strings as trustee of Vicky's inheritance. But Jeff, by the Wodehouse code, can't marry and be an heiress's kept man;

5. has not allowed for an 'all-our-troubles-are-over' love scene for Jeff and Vicky;

6. has not yet 'planted' Brenda's bracelet (or necklace), the stealing of which is to bring down the curtain on Act 2, so to speak, and provide good alarums and excursions at the beginning of the final Act;

7. has scarcely touched on the necessary romance of Sergeant Murchison and Marilyn Poole. That chauffeur, of whom Murchison is jealous, is a dark horse. Will he be developed?

8. has left Brenda, Piper's sister, at a loose end. It is not like the benign Wodehouse to leave even such an unrewarding character as Brenda unrewarded with an autumn romance of her own. After all, Constance, who has harassed, bullied and dominated Lord Emsworth

from book to book, story to story, is allowed to marry two nice American millionaires successively. And the awful Roderick Spode, in the Bertie Wooster books, has his Madeline Bassett to dream about. Brenda, in this book, would surely be smiling when last seen. And her brother's successful courtship of Diana will not be enough to keep that smile on her face for long. James and Diana are *not* likely to want her to come and live with them at Number 11 Downing Street;

9. has not settled whether the Empress's portrait is going to please Lord Emsworth this time and, if so, whether he will hang it triumphantly in the family portrait gallery or have it, less triumphantly, in his study.

We are back in a favourite Blandings theme — the heroine brought to the castle to keep her away, and cool her off, from the penniless hero; the infiltration of the castle by the hero in some guise, organized by Galahad (or Lord Ickenham); the weaving of the web of deceit, false names, false purposes, 'telling the tale'; the recognition scene (impostor unmasked, 'never darken these doors again', etc.); the theft of something valuable (Lord Emsworth's pig, Gally's Memoirs, Aunt Connie's, or this time Brenda's, necklace) which, being found and restored, makes the just rejoice, the unjust look silly and the right couples able to marry happily.

How to get the heroine's loved one into the castle without the fierce hostess (any of Lord Emsworth's sisters will do) knowing that he is the man the heroine is here to forget — this is the recurrent problem in the beginnings of Blandings novels and stories. It is no good letting Lord Emsworth into the conspiracy. He would sooner or later give it away, by mistake, to his sister. So he has to be fooled too. In this novel, Wodehouse is toying with, not to say muddling, two ideas, both of which he has used before: the infiltration of the castle by the hero as an artist to paint the Empress, as Bill Lister in *Full Moon*, or as a candidate for the job of Lord Emsworth's secretary, as Jerry Vail in *Pigs Have Wings*.

But for some reason Gally tells Claude Duff that Jeff is at the castle trying for the secretary job when Jeff is already installed as the artist to paint the Empress.

As the last sentence of Chapter 16 shows, Vicky has some minutes' start on Gally and must act without his advice. Gally has only just learnt that Florence has rumbled Jeff's alias. Vicky has had time to remove a necklace from the jewel case that Brenda has carelessly left in the hall. Her purpose is to delay, if not prevent, Jeff's being given marching orders by his hostess, her step-mother. No suspect will be allowed to leave the castle until the necklace is found, and Jeff is without doubt going to be suspected.

Vicky tells Gally that she has pinched the necklace, and she gives it to him. He puts it in some obvious place in Lord Emsworth's study. Brenda discovers the loss of the necklace and sure enough the finger of suspicion points to Jeff, by now known to be Vicky's demon lover, in need of money, and here under an assumed name. Florence and Brenda decide to ask Claude Duff to search Jeff's room for the necklace. Jeff still doesn't know that Brenda and Florence know that he is an impostor, let alone that they have told Vicky that he is to be kicked out of the castle immediately. He does not know anything about any necklace, nor that Vicky has stolen it to make it inconvenient for 'them' to kick him out.

Gally tells Lord Emsworth that Florence is kicking out the man who is, at last, painting his beloved pig's portrait, and is anyway his, Lord Emsworth's, guest. This is where Lord Emsworth begins to see red and become the dominant male. He slates Brenda for having put Claude on to search a guest's room. Brenda goes and complains to

Florence, and while she slates him for having been rude to Brenda, he slates her for attempting to kick Jeff out.

Now, here comes Florence's husband. Inspired by Ovens's home-brew beer and urged on by Galahad, he has been sneaked into the castle and intends to plead with his estranged wife. So he has hidden himself in a cupboard in her room. He hears Lord Emsworth slating her, and he emerges in his wrath from the cupboard and, pending his appeal to Florence, he wades into Lord Emsworth for his harsh words to her. When Florence gets over her shock at seeing her husband (Kevin) again and coming out of a cupboard, she stands amazed, as Lord Emsworth does, too, by the man's courage in giving Lord Emsworth the rough of his tongue.

Lord Emsworth leaves Florence's room, shaking his head. But he returns for a moment to say, 'Is this the necklace you're all making such a lot of trouble about? I found it in my study. Very careless to leave it about, whoever did.'

Florence and Brenda leave the castle in a fury against Lord Emsworth and Gally and Jeff. They take Kevin with them, and he will henceforth dominate railway porters, head-waiters and the actors in, and the producers of, his instantly successful plays. He will also dominate the willing Florence, his ever-to-be-loving wife. But his first act of dominance over her has been to persuade her to give her blessing to Vicky and Jeff's marriage and to release Vicky's money to her. It was Gally who helped Kevin to re-win his wife and Kevin owes it to Gally to fix that for him. And, if we worry that Lord Emsworth may still be suffering from shock after being bawled out by Kevin, we should remember the end of *A Pelican at Blandings*. There Lord Emsworth, in the thick of battle for 200 pages, has forgotten everybody and everything within a few days of being left in peace, perfect peace, alone with Gally in his own castle.

It would create a bit of a problem in Wodehouse's strict code of morals if Vicky and Jeff were left together at the end of this book, chaperoned only by males (Lord Emsworth, Gally and Beach). But this is where we pick up Claude Duff. An early sequence of Wodehouse's notes shows that he had Claude Duff (at that stage Claude Winkworth) pencilled in as a major, rather than a minor, character:

Secretary

Claude Winkworth
Crushed from childhood by being ordinary son of illustrious parents.

Aunt, Dame Daphne: Father, the eminent historian, Professor Ernest W: Uncle, novelist Alistair W: Sister, Claudine [. . ? . .] Shakespearean actress: Mother, artist.

Much too tall for his width.

Claude accosts Gally because he feels he must cure himself of shyness.

Why is Jeff Claude's hero? At school together. Jeff athlete, always treated him as equal. At Cambridge, Rugger blue.

In the typescript first draft Claude is minor, and he suffers, in terms of Wodehouse characterization, from good looks. He is rich, well dressed, a pianist, a bachelor and a great success with the girls. And—and this has always, in Wodehouse's books, spelt r-o-t-t-e-r—he is very handsome. And now he has fallen in love with Vicky, not knowing of her love for his old friend, and hero, Jeff, or of Jeff's for Vicky.

Wodehouse would have developed Claude and found a much fuller purpose for him than has so far been revealed. My own bet is that Claude would have lost his good looks, either by their being simply omitted from the preliminary sketch or, the hard way, as Hollywood's Mike Cardinal did in *Spring Fever*, by getting his face re-arranged in some honourable fight or scuffle. Claude would then have been built up in two or three good scenes, at least one of them retroactively to the first half of the book.

My guess is, then, that in an early chapter Vicky had begged to be allowed to ask a school friend to come and stay with her in her captivity. And this her step-mother was only too glad to grant. Now, though everybody had forgotten about her, this girl arrives. She is welcomed by all as providing a modicum of chaperonage for Vicky when Diana goes back with Sir James, taking Murchison, Marilyn and Claude Duff with them. But there is just time, before they go, for Claude to lose his heart as suddenly to Vicky's friend as he did to Vicky. So he doesn't go back with his boss. Sir James, in a yeastly benevolence as a result of his own approaching nuptials, gives Claude indefinite leave.

So Jeff stays on and finishes the Empress's portrait, with Vicky in the background during working hours. Claude and Vicky's friend stay on the premises too. And then, in addition to the portraits that Jeff is asked to paint, of Sir James Piper for a start and then, Gally hopes, of all the other members of the Cabinet, Claude gets Jeff the job of Advertising Manager of Duff & Trotter, where the money is good and steady and he can pay his whack with Vicky as man and wife.

The Empress's portrait, we all wish to think, will now hang in the family portrait gallery. Lord Emsworth can enjoy looking at it whenever he is not out at the sty looking at its sitter. Gally and Beach ring down the curtain over a glass or two of port in the pantry. Beach is now distantly step-related to Gally (and Lord Emsworth, Florence, Connie and all the other eight sisters), but he will continue to be the supreme butler. McAllister is still head gardener, though his cousin married Freddie Threepwood. And Beach's niece, Maudie Stubbs (Maudie Montrose of the Criterion bar) is, we have reason to believe, Lady Parsloe at Matchingham Hall, just across the fields from the castle. She might indeed have been Lord Emsworth's second Countess if Jerry Vail hadn't retrieved that ardent letter from and for his master in *Pigs Have Wings*. Had that sudden infatuation led to the altar, Lord Emsworth would have been calling his butler 'Uncle Sebastian'. For many books now Beach has been butler at the castle 'for eighteen years'. Lady Constance has tried to sack him or get him pensioned off. At least twice he has tendered his own resignation. I think that Wodehouse must here have wanted to give Beach 'tenure', a hoop of steel binding him to the family, a seat for life in the Upper House.

Have we left anybody out? Yes, Freddie Threepwood, and purposely. In this first draft he only threatens to come to the castle. He doesn't come. It's a threat because, if he did come, he would certainly blow the gaff on his old friend Jeff's imposture, as he did for Bill Lister's in *Full Moon*. No. That journey of Gally's to London in the Bentley just to warn Freddie off—that will come out. Freddie will remain 'off' and threaten nobody in this last book. The bad news that he hasn't been able to sell Jeff's strip cartoon in America, or the good news that he has sold it (Wodehouse tries it both ways in his notes), can be telephoned to the castle. Wodehouse is going to need all the space he can get now, to tie up existing loose ends and to add the flesh and muscle to the bare bones of the narrative as it will stand when he has given the last six chapters the same treatment as the first sixteen.

*

That is my guess, based on the January 19th 1975 scenario, at how Chapters 17–22 might have run. What

we have read in Chapters 1–16 is the first typescript of
two-thirds of a novel by a great professional humorist of
ninety-three. Ninety-three. The remaining work might
have taken Wodehouse weeks, or months. But once a
scenario was leak-proof, with couples coupled and loners
left happily alone, Wodehouse put together his first rough
typescript and reckoned his main labour and slog-work
was over. There remained the part he really enjoyed:
revising, cutting, adding, adding, adding, shaping,
smoothing to a high polish.

Evelyn Waugh was an outspoken admirer of Wodehouse's writings, and Wodehouse admired much of
Waugh's. Waugh had a nearly complete set of Wodehouse,
bound in leather. He was one of the many who were
prepared to refer to Wodehouse as 'The Master'. Frances
Donaldson, who knew the Wodehouses, but is not quite a
devotee of Wodehouse's writings, says, in her book on
Evelyn Waugh, that she questioned Waugh about 'the
Master stuff'. He replied, 'One has to regard a man as a
Master who can produce on average three uniquely
brilliant and entirely original similes to each page.'

Wodehouse's trained mind was a fat thesaurus of
quotations, jargons and images: clichés in their proper
contexts but, misapplied and mismated by him, jewels.
Uniquely brilliant, yes; entirely original, yes, when he
gave himself time to revise, comb and brush to a fine gloss.
I say 'comb' because in early stages his plots could fall into
familiar knots, and he sometimes repeated, from previous
books or in the same book, his own felicities of image or
phrase.

I still hold that, paragraph by paragraph, simile by
simile, sentence by sentence and phrase by phrase, *Joy in
the Morning* (1947) is Wodehouse's most *brilliant* book, and
I am sure I know the simple reason why. It was the one he
had worked on longest. He did it in two stretches, one at
Le Touquet when the war had started, but before the

Germans came and sent him to internment (up to that moment he had got *Joy in the Morning* to just beyond the stage that this novel, *Sunset at Blandings*, is in, with four chapters to go instead of, as here, six). The second stretch started eleven months later, when his wife brought the manuscript to him in Germany, where they were re-united, all four of them (Wodehouse, Ethel Wodehouse, Wonder the pekingese and the manuscript of *Joy in the Morning*), on his release from Tost Camp. *Joy in the Morning* is a book that he was able to finish, revise, comb, polish and re-polish in his enforced retirement, with no deadline from any publisher looming. Practically every sentence in the book has a glow in it. It represented three or four years of intermittent and always fresh work. His average for a novel up till then had been a year, with interruptions.

In the case of the sixteen chapters here, revision would (to alter slightly the plastered Gussie Fink-Nottle's phrasing in his speech to those Market Snodsbury school kids in *Right Ho, Jeeves*) be taking out as well as a putting in. Wodehouse knew he repeated himself in old age. He had to watch out for it more carefully. Incidentally, one of the good stories in his own autobiographical repertoire is of going, when young and gauche, to a lunch-party at W. S. Gilbert's table. Gilbert started on an involved anecdote and all his guests waited for the punch-line. Young Wodehouse didn't wait long enough, laughed too early, murdered his host's story and good humour, and generally disgraced himself. But to one man at the table Wodehouse's gaffe brought delight—the butler who had had to listen to his master telling the same story so often before. 'Writhing with embarrassment, I caught the eye of the butler, and I shall never forget the dog-like devotion in it' (*Bring on the Girls*).

To those who are sporadic readers of Wodehouse, all the sixteen chapters here may read fresh as well as good.

Those who know the Wodehouse canon almost by heart will see that of the two hundred, say, verbal felicities here, twenty or so would have been removed from the final draft, discarded as not freshly minted: 'den of the Secret Nine', 'saying Bo to a goose', 'drained the bitter cup only to find a dead mouse at the bottom', 'Lord Emsworth drooping like a wet sock', 'baronets need watching', 'Sherlock Holmes could have taken her correspondence course', 'had he not been seated he would undoubtedly have drawn himself up to his full height'.

They are few, and they were roses when he first showed them. He would have cast them out as yesterday's blooms had he been spared the time. And, in the natural course of fleshing out the barebones script, he would have added many more, new ones. In its unfinished state *Sunset at Blandings* has given us a chance, more recent and more detailed than *Performing Flea* (1953) did, to see the professional at work.

He wouldn't have much liked the idea of people looking over his shoulder at his working notes, still less trying to write his missing last chapters. His notes, he would have thought, wouldn't have made much sense to anybody else anyway. Often they made no sense at all to him. We are privileged here to be reading what was strictly his business.

*

It is clear that the idea of a Cabinet Minister and his guard had been bumping round in Wodehouse's mind for years. In December 1976 there came up for sale by auction at Sotheby's in Chancery Lane two items, described in the catalogue as follows:

The Property of a Lady

602 WODEHOUSE (Sir PELHAM GRENVILLE) DRAFT OF HIS NOVEL 'MUCH OBLIGED, JEEVES', opening:

As I parked myself at the breakfast table that morning, and started to dig into the toothsome eggs and bacon which Jeeves had given of his plenty, I took a quick glance at the world and liked the look of it. Not a flaw in the setup, it seemed to me.

"Jeeves," I said, "I am happy today."

"I am very glad to hear it, sir." . . .

c. 170 pages of typescript with extensive autograph revisions, c. 10 pages of autograph text, with over 50 pages of mostly autograph 'scenario' notes interspersed through the text, c. 250 pages in all, loose, 4to

∴ *Much Obliged Jeeves* was published in 1971. The present draft is dated in one place 9 August 1970. INCLUDED IN THE LOT IS A VOLUME OF AUTOGRAPH WORKING NOTES FOR THE NOVEL, *c. 50 pages, the recto of the tenth leaf marked by Wodehouse: "This is where the notes for MUCH OBLIGED, JEEVES start", in a 'Criterion' school note-book, upper cover inscribed "Jeeves Notes", 4to.*

603 WODEHOUSE (P.G.) DRAFT OF HIS NOVEL 'GUESTS AT THE CASTLE (A BLANDINGS CASTLE NOVEL)', opening:

The summer day was drawing to a close and dusk had fallen on Blandings Castle, shrouding from view the ancient battlements, dulling the silver surface of the lake and causing that supreme Berkshire sow Empress of Blandings to leave the open air portion of her sty and withdraw into the covered shed which formed her sleeping quarters. A dedicated believer in the maxim of early to bed and early to rise, she always turned in at about this time. Only by getting its regular eight hours can a pig keep up to the mark and preserve that schoolgirl complexion . . .

c. 250 pages of typescript with extensive autograph revisions and an autograph title-sheet, loose, 4to.

∴ INCLUDED WITH THE PRESENT DRAFT ARE C. 130 PAGES

OF AUTOGRAPH WORKING-NOTES variously headed "Cabinet Minister and Guard Novel" and "Blandings Novel", dated between December 1966 and May 1968, *loose, 4to.*

As a matter of record, Lot 602 was sold for £1,000, Lot 603 for £900. As a matter of interest, when a similar bundle of typescript and autograph notes, for *Jeeves in the Offing*, had come up in a sale for charity at Sotheby's in 1959, it had gone to a New York dealer for £100.

I was particularly interested, this time, in Number 603. *Guests at the Castle* eventually got changed to *A Pelican at Blandings*, as you may recognize from that opening paragraph. Parts of the draft were cut, other parts re-located and many of the revisions were re-revised before it all came to print in 1969. But more particularly I wanted to see the working notes for that story that he had headed *Cabinet Minister and Guard Novel*. Surely that could be, surely that is, a foretaste of the novel we've got here in 1977?

No. It's not as easy as that. The first entry, hand-written in red ink, dated November 23rd 1967, reads:

Try this :–
Hero loves ward in chancery.
Lord Chancellor won't give consent.
Lord Chancellor infatuated with some girl.
Girl makes him go in for strenuous athletics
Elderly woman tells him he's crazy wooing young girl
He won't listen to her. He writes to her proposing.
Some scene where girl makes him do something which
    exhausts him (e.g. riding)
He goes off girl. How to recover letter?
Hero recovers letter and gets consent to marry heroine.
Lord Chancellor marries elderly woman.

Where's the guard in that? He has been dismissed already. But characters flickering to and fro in pages following begin to suggest to Wodehouse's mind that the Blandings scenery would do for the story, and many of the Blandings costumes. The notes drift away from the Lord Chancellor, and Blandings through the mists rises into towers. It is going to be a Blandings novel. Lord Emsworth is there, wishing he was alone. But Lady Constance is there, and the Duke of Dunstable, and Uncle Fred.

And here the Lord Chancellor comes back:

Nov 29th 1967

Try this. Ld Ch sees Empress & is fascinated, as he is a pig breeder. He offers to buy her. Ld E appalled. Ld E consults Uncle Fred (or Gally), who says he knows Ld Ch of old as a man who sticks at nothing, and says imperative to get a tec immediately to watch Ld Ch. He looks in Classified Telephone Directory. The name on top is J. Sheringham Adair.

I think it wd be funny if Gally (or UF) told Beach to go and engage Chimp.

Chimp comes as friend of Ld E (son of old friend?) or pig expert, much to indignation of Lady C.

I think Beach wd make Chimp shave his moustache.

Try this. At end of story UF tells Lady C that he is a little surprised at her leaving Schoonmaker alone in New York. He has known S all his life & he knows no more sterling character, but he is so amiable that he might quite easily get entangled with some woman. ('You see how Ld C did' 'But S is not like Ld C.' 'No. No, of course not, but—'). This makes Lady C leave in a hurry.

Then a final little scene of Ld E and UF at Empress's sty, feeling how nice it is to be alone.

Good. No. Better have UF draw a poignant picture of Schoon's loneliness).

Try this. Dolly gets idea of stealing pig so that Soapy can restore it and get in good with Ld E. Soapy is afraid of pig; so D. starts to steal it & gets in some

trouble, which UF gets her out of. Or else she falls foul of Chimp and beans him, and Chimp tells UF that D is Mrs. Soapy.Φ
Φ *This is all v. vague at present. Work on it.*)
X Soapy shd somehow get in bad with Ld. E.

Then, after many intervening pages:

Dec 1 1967

Does the Lord Chancellor have a secret service guardian?

Dolly tells Soapy it's lucky they made her his daughter, as she confidently expects to sell Ld C oil stock.
Good)

In their first scene she tells him that a v. big pot is arriving—the Ld Ch of England.
This plants Ld C. Lady C has referred to him as George X, and she has been told by UF that he is Ld Ch.
Good)

Try this. Hero is composer or lyrist with a big show coming on on B'way. He asks Ld Ch for consent— refused as income uncertain. Then cable comes saying show smash. He looks for Ld Ch to tell him & is interrupted by Lady C, who kicks him out.
V Good XX)

Instead of Ld Ch's guard make it George, Ld E's grandson, who takes a violent fancy to Ld Ch and never leaves him—cp Denis the Menace & Mr Wolson [?].

The last entry, under the dateline April 13th 1968, is:

For end try this:
1. Duke gives Lord E letter
2. Next day UF goes to see Duke.+ Lady C, says she has had letter from Schoonmaker saying he can't get to England, so she is returning to America. She adds about Mother losing her memory [? money]—Lady C.

Duke tells UF about letter. UF is sympathetic, but has nothing to suggest.

X)

3. Mother leaves [. . ? . . .] UF meets Lord E, who says he has just found letter in his pocket. UF goes to Duke, says he told John abt letter. John recovered it. How I don't know. He has his secret methods. Duke says give it to me. UF says about John losing Linda and won't give up letter till Duke has written consent to marriage. *This looks nearly right*)

*

In 1967/8 Wodehouse was a mere eighty-six, rising eighty-seven. In March three years later he is jotting down another suggestion for a novel:

Middle aged man in love with energetic girl
He has old Nanny who looks on him as a child.
She notes his wooing and disapproves of it. (Master Willie)
Make him Cabinet Minister with policeman guarding him (see *An English Crime*).
Every time he is about to propose, he sees cops watching . . .

That novel died unborn.

Wodehouse hadn't thought of a title for this last Blandings novel that you have just read. Or rather, he thought of fifteen and jotted them down in the sidelines of various pages of notes:

> *Lord Emsworth Entertains*
> *Blandings Castle Fills Up*
> *Gally to the Rescue*
> *The Weird Old Buster*
> *All's Well at Blandings*
> *Trouble at Blandings Castle*

Gally Takes Charge
Unrest at Blandings Castle
Gally in Charge
Rely on Gally
Leave it to Galahad
The Helping Hand of Galahad
Life with Galahad
Women are Peculiar
Love at the Castle

The title he would *not* have given the novel is *Sunset at Blandings*. That was suggested, with subtle daring, by either Mr. Chatto or Mr. Windus and agreed instantly by the other. It is apt. But Wodehouse himself would never have locked, even if only by suggestion, the great gates of the castle. He would have wanted it there, with its sun high in the sky, for another visit if the mood took him, to incarcerate another pretty girl, dispatched, or brought, by another (what, another? That would make eleven) Threepwood sister to the Bastille, to be followed by another nephew or protégé of Galahad's or Lord Ickenham's under a false name.

*

Wodehouse would have been ninety-four in October 1975. He had been knighted in the New Year's Honours list. He had been Sir Pelham Wodehouse for forty-six days when he died. He had gone into the Southampton hospital on Long Island for tests to find out the cause and cure of a troublesome skin-rash. He hated hospitals, but, as for the last three-quarters of a century, he could forget the world anywhere as long as he had plenty of pencils, pens and paper, a typewriter, a pipe or two, tobacco and, for occasional pauses, a pile of detective novels. He had all these, except the typewriter, with him in the hospital and he had been working on this novel on the morning of

February 14th. He died that evening, of a heart attack. It was Valentine's Day. The American flag above the Post Office at Remsenburg, where the Wodehouses had lived for the last fifteen and more years, was lowered to half-mast, barely clearing the piled up snow beneath it.

On the typescript of the sixteen chapters there are, in increasingly difficult handwriting, a number of free-standing corrections and additions. These have been incorporated here. In a few places Wodehouse had decided that he had gone off the rails and the sequences needed to be re-worked and re-written. Against these he may have put a cross (X) and the word 'Fix'. Those passages have not been 'fixed' here, but you can see where he wanted immediate changes if you study that January 19th 1975 scenario.

The thirty-three pages of notes that were found in the hospital almost all looked forward to the end of the book. Only seven of them had date-lines at their head: those of June 10th 1974, June 22nd, November 2nd, December 20th, December 30th, January 9th 1975 and January 19th.

These were the hundred and twenty-three pages, type-script and notes, collected from the hospital, that were offered to Chatto & Windus in November 1976—the last Wodehouse novel, albeit incomplete and in an unpolished form, and thirty-three pages of notes with a suggestion for the ending. But it soon became obvious to us that there must have been, and probably still existed somewhere, many more pages of notes. Thirty-three was a fraction of the number of pages Wodehouse had covered with notes for previous novels. Happily, further papers did come to light in Remsenburg and from these I was able to identify another one hundred and fifty autograph pages which clearly had something to do with this novel. The names, Jeff, Vicky, Piper, Gally, Florence, Beach, Blandings— these sprang to meet the eye.

I have not been able to piece the newly retrieved pages

into any certain sequence. Ten of them are dated, and their sequence is June 10th 1974, June 12th, June 13th, June 14th, June 25th, June 26th, June 27th, June 28th, August 3rd and January 16th 1975. This shows that it wasn't just his last thirty-three pages of notes that Wodehouse took with him to the hospital with the typescript. The earliest date on a page found in the study at home is the same (June 10th 1974) as the earliest date on a page Wodehouse had with him in the hospital. And the page headed January 16th 1975 was found in the study.

Of the remaining, undated, pages, some show themselves to be early rather than late. For different periods in the early stages of the build-up to this novel, for instance, Jeff and Vicky are still 'hero' and heroine', and the 'heroine' gets named Nicky at first, and sometimes even after 'Vicky' has come in. The Chancellor of the Exchequer starts as the Lord Chancellor, Florence starts as Dora, Claude Duff as Claude Winkworth. There are three such clues visible in the page dated June 14th 1974 (page 129). Sometimes a train of thought links two or three pages. Sometimes a note refers specifically to the number of a page in the typescript. It is probably fair to assume that notes building towards a sequence in Chapter 10, say, of the typescript were written before notes that can be referred to something in Chapter 15. Fair, but not absolutely safe. The handwriting itself sometimes suggests a link between one page and another, seldom more than that. But, if there is enough textual evidence in those hundred and eighty-three pages of notes for a scholar to establish a chronologically sure 1–183 pagination, I am not that scholar. And I am sure that one hundred and eighty-three is not the total that Wodehouse had written.

What we have in sum is a treasure trove: a rough narrative of two-thirds of a novel, and a hoard of good insights into Wodehouse's method of composition: his ideas for the ending, his dry runs at passages later given temporary approval in typescript under the stamp of 'Aziz', his criticisms of his own jotted-down notes.

We have given a wide sample of the note pages. We have put them into type as plainly as possible. When you study the reproductions, which have been reduced from $8\frac{1}{2}'' \times 11''$, you will see that we have been faced with difficulties. We have done our best.

Wodehouse's personal shorthand for 'Enter' was 'plus' or '+'; for 'Exit' it was 'minus' or '—'. Thus, 'Plus Ld E—F' would be 'Enter Lord Emsworth, exit Florence'. Wodehouse's 'Aziz' means 'Leave it as it is for now'. He used Φ as a signal to a note below or in the margin. So also Δ (once). Italic in the transcript here means a word, or words, underlined by Wodehouse; or it is a marginal note or other addition, made apparently at the time of writing. Marginalia are indicated in the transcribed pages by a single round bracket. Square brackets indicate my interpolations. Thus [... ? ...] means that there is a handwritten word that I cannot read. **Bold type** (like that) means a Wodehouse postscript in the margin or in the text, usually in red ink.

We have transcribed all the datelined pages of the Wodehouse notes and given a number of them, with a few others, in reproduction. Note (e.g. under date June 10th 1974) that in transcription we have not always omitted, or indicated, words and lines that Wodehouse crossed out.

Two beginnings, later discarded, are echoing through the first datelined pages. In one, when Gally arrives at the castle, some of the castle's inhabitants (not Lord Emsworth) have gone to have lunch at a neighbour's house where they meet a fascinating, fine, rich and unattached lady, sister of the Lord Chancellor. In another, there has been a fire at a (or the) neighbour's house and Lord Emsworth's sister Dora (who later becomes Florence, and later still Diana) proposes to ask all the inhabitants and guests there to come and stay at the castle pending repairs.

*

There follow transcriptions of the datelined pages in the order of their calendar dates:

June 10. 1974

1. Try this. Gally arrives at Blandings, expecting to find Lord Emsworth alone and the castle is full. Ld E explains about Dora and the fire. (Sn At sty)

Good)

There are at Castle Chancellor of Exchequer, rich woman (his sister?), and Chancellor's nephew (heroine's friend), Dora and her daughter, heroine. Also hero? And bodyguard

2. It might be better if Gally first meets Beach and goes to sty to comfort Ld E. Finds Ld E with hero.

Good)

3. The household is lunching out. When they return, heroine goes to welcome Gally, who is a great pal of hers.

She tells him about meeting hero, whom she knew as a kid, and getting him the job. Plug that she thinks he is hard up.

She tells him she is engaged. Gally dubious?

Heroine not at lunch party. She was out when Gally arrived)

At lunch the party met rich American girl and fiancé realised she was good thing and told heroine he would have to be leaving. He breaks engt? (Then girl's father loses his money)

Good)

When heroine catches hero breaking in & beans him, she has come down stairs to get a drink, having had shock of finding letter from fiancé, breaking engt. (Or

does he tell her? Cd·he tell her he has lost all his
money on Stock Exch?)

Query: After dinner Dora tells Gally not to monopolize
'fine' woman, as she intends that Ld E shall marry her?
Good)

Plant Gally having known bodyguard's father.

End Act One with heroine finding letter.

*

June 10/74

Ld E must not get onto Dora wanting him to marry the woman till later in the story.

Problem

Heroine can't be in love with another man. It makes her seem too shallow if she abruptly switches to hero. **See June 15.**

I must get heroine in love with hero, and he in danger of being chucked out for some reason.

What then is heroine's idea in pinching jewel?

What does she gain if he stays on?

Hero's threatened departure ought to be connected with Chancellor.

Am I wrong in making hero artist come to paint pig? **No** It looks as if the best plan would be to make heroine be Chancellor's daughter (*or trustee*). Hero and she quarrel. Why? Hero abuses Chan and heroine ticks him off and hero says he's leaving. She knows that if they stay together, she can bring him round.

No Or cd Chan be trustee to hero? Or wd that be too like Aunts Aren't Gentlemen?

Or cd Chancellor (who in this case wd be Labour man) want hero to go into his business? Finding that hero is painting pig, he delivers an ultimatum & hero rebels. Heroine ticks him off.

Then Heroine wd *not* be Dora's daughter.

Good)

This looks the best so far.

*

June 12/74

When heroine meets Gally in scenario of June 10, she could tell him hero has sent comic strip to America. (Then at end he reveals that it has been accepted) Who is heroine?

Good)

126

She cd be daughter of old friend of Gally's. Cd she have
been secty to Ld E?

CHARACTERS

1. Chancellor of Exchequer
2. His Sister
3. Ld Emsworth

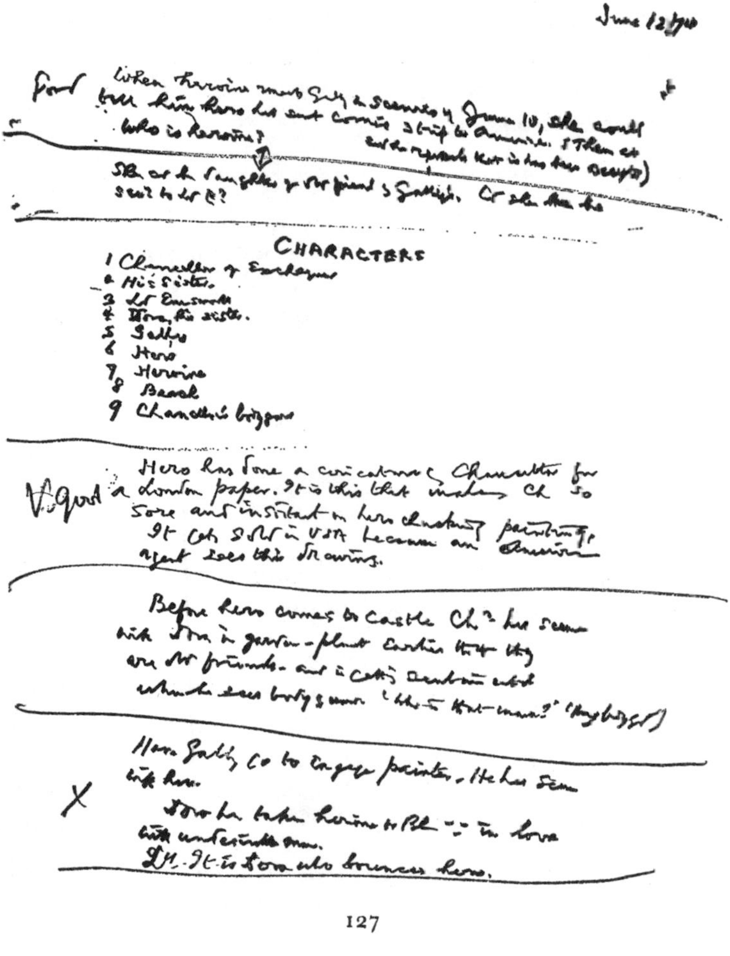

June 12/40

Good when heroine must Gally & scandal of June 10, she could
well kiss how has sent corns stuff to America. & Then ask
who is heroine? and to reproach her is has been occupy?
She or h [unclear] or her friend's English. Or she then he
sent to Ld E?

CHARACTERS

1 Chancellor of Exchequer
2 His Sister.
3 Lt Emsworth
4 Wora, his sister.
5 Sally
6 Hero
7 Heroine
8 Baxah
9 Chancellor's bodyguard

Good Hero has done a caricature of Chancellor for
a London paper. It is this that makes Ch so
sore and insistent on her checking painting.
It cd sell in USA because an American
agent sees this drawing.

Before hero comes to Castle Ch & he seem
nice John in guardian-plant curtice that they
are not friends. and in Ch's dealings what
which ends bitty sunn. "the [unclear] that—man?" (heybody's)

Have Sally go to engage painter. He has seen
nice him.
John he takes heroine to Bl — in love
with understand man.
LM. It is John who bounces hero.

127

4. Dora, his sister
5. Gally
6. Hero
7. Heroine
8. Beach
9. Chancellor's bodyguard

Hero has done a caricature of Chancellor for a London paper. It is this that makes Ch so sore and insistant on hero chucking painting.
It gets sold in USA because an American agent sees this drawing.
V. Good)

Before hero comes to castle Ch has scene with Dora in garden — plant earlier that they are old friends and is getting sentimental when he sees bodyguard.
'Who is that man?' 'My bodyguard'

Have Gally go to engage painter. He has scene with hero. Dora has taken heroine to Bl ⁚ in love with undesirable man.
Qr. It is Dora who bounces hero.
X)

*

June 13/74
It was of Galahad Threepwood that his niece X had said — quote abt his being so fit.

Sequence

1. Gally arrives at castle, expecting to find Ld E alone. Beach tells him Dora and daughter are there. Dora and heroine are lunching out.
2. Gally goes to sty. Ld E tells him heroine has fallen in love with undesirable man.
3. Gally meets heroine. She tells him hero is an artist.

Gally says Ld E was talking of getting artist to paint pig. He will get hero the job.

4. Gally meets Dora. She says old flame of hers staying at lunch house.

5. Gally goes to see hero. (Son of old friend).

6. The fire. Dora is going to invite the 'lunch' people to stay. She says sister of Chancellor knew Ld E as young man & tells G. not to monopolize her, as she is going to try to marry her to Ld E. Φ Plant here that she used to know Chr well.

Gally goes to Ld E and warns him . . . No.

7. Scene in grounds. Chr and Dora. He is getting sentimental, when he sees bodyguard: 'Who is that man?' 'My bodyguard!'

8. Cut to hero.

Φ Here should come a scene at sty, when the 'fire house' woman calls the Empress revolting. It is after this that Gally warns Ld E. (Probably the scene when Dora tells Gally she is going to get Ld E married cd be better played off stage.

Query: Make the woman v. political — strong on people's rights. She has never met Ld E and takes him for the pig man. She rebukes him for servility — intelligent man like you degrading yourself by acting as valet to a revolting pig.

Good)

Note: Shall I delay her arrival, so that this scene cd come nearer end?

*

June 14, 1974

Work on 6 of June 12 [?13]. The Ld E-Woman scene ought to lead to something.

Start with Dora telling Gally not to monopolize Ch's sister, who is coming later. Note. The fire cd be at a house in next county, and sister have stopped on in

London to see about insurance. (Dora reads the news in her paper).

Sister & Ld E. She says natives in Uganda are starving and you shovel food into this revolting pig. Ld E might have retorted that the n of U probably wd not enjoy the Emp's menu which as evbod knows consists [...?...] too much aghast to speak & she walks on.

Sister walks on, meets hero. She must know him. (How?) She goes back to house and meets Dora. She says she met hero. I've forgotten his name. Dora says X. No that wasn't it. Ha yes, it was Y, mentioning hero's real name, Dora appalled.
Dora tackles hero, kicks him out.
Hero tells heroine, who gets idea of stealing jewel.
Good)

Heroine steals jewel.
Dora discovers loss.
Dora tells Chancellor.
Bodyguard appears from behind curtain.
Nobody must leave this house. Then Ld E takes hero to pig. Hero shut out climbs in and *sister* beans him.
Good)

Then 'sister' becomes 'tec.

Sister & bodyguard. Sister suspects hero.
Meanwhile, Gally has given Ld E [... ? ... ...? ...]
They decide to return it.
Gally caught by bodyguard. G. knew his father

*

June 14/74
I can't get any further till I get the end of story, and it must be something clever that Gally does so as to force Dora to consent to hero & heroine marrying.

Cd he somehow work it that he makes it seem that

Ld E is guilty of the theft? In that case, jewel shd be 'sister's'.

B

Try this. Heroine steals jewel in order to keep hero in house.

Gally hides it by putting it in Ld E's study, (without Ld

June 14/[19

I can't get any further till I get the end of story, and it must be something clever that Gally does so as to force Dora to consent to hero + heroine marrying.

Or he somehow work so that he makes it seem that Ld E is guilty of the theft? In that case, jewel shd be 'sister's'.

B

Try this. Heroine steals jewel in order to keep hero in house. Gally hides it by putting it in Ld E's study, (without Ld E's knowledge). He shows it to Dora and says Ld E has obviously acted kleptomania to his eccentricities. If this is discovered, his name will be mud, so Ch⁴ won't marry Dora. (He says shd I tell him so now (v. attract by law.)

I want to make it plausible that he makes terms as hero + heroine for his sister. Not-right-but-work on it.

A

① No. Try this, to make it continuous. Ch⁴ tells Gally he wants to propose to Dora but can't because s bodyguard. Gally puts bodyguard out of action in a comic scene. Dora comes to Gally and says she is engaged to Ch⁴. Gally says At this joyful time you will want to spread happiness, give your consent to him + heroine and persuade Ld to give him his money. Dora says he (expects his still reason for further reason). G. says "If you won't, you won't, but come with me, I want to show you something."

God

Then as in A B

✗ End book with G + Brock chatting.

E's knowledge). He shows it to Dora and says Ld E has obviously added kleptomania to his eccentricities. If this is discovered, his name will be mud. Ld Chr won't marry Dora. (**He says Ld E told him he was v. attracted by her**).

I want to make it plausible that he makes terms re hero & heroine for his silence.

Not right yet but work on it.

X)

A

Try this, to make it continuous. Chr tells Gally he wants to propose to Dora but can't because of bodyguard. Gally puts bodyguard out of action in a comic scene. Dora comes to Gally and says she is engaged to Chr: Gally says At this joyful time you will want to spread happiness, give your consent to hero and heroine and persuade Chr to give hero his money. Dora says No (ought to have solid reason for disliking hero). G says 'If you won't, you won't, but come with me, I want to show you something: Then as in B

No. Cut trustee idea. Dora says hero has no money. G says hero has comic strip in USA.)

Good)

End book with G & Beach chatting.

X)

*

June 22 1974

Ch. 1. Jno Robinson's taxi, which meets all the trains at Market Blandings, drew up with a screeching of brakes at the great door of Bl Castle, Lord E's seat in Shropshire, and a dapper little man of middle age alighted with the agile abandon of a cat on hot bricks. This, as any number the old brigade could have told you, was the Hon. Galahad Threepwood Ld E's younger brother. **[all deleted]**

132

2. Plant housemaid with whom bodyguard falls in love.

Murchison is sick of seeing Sir James
Their politics are opposite it is agony for him to have to listen to J's speeches.

X)

Mechanism for Gally getting bodyguard out of the way. In Ch 1 Beach tells Gally housemaid (his niece?) is

being wooed by bodyguard. He doesn't approve?
Good)
So when Ld Ch tells him his story he goes to bodyguard
and advises him to take housemaid by storm.
'I wd die for one little rose from her hair.
'Has she got roses in her hair?
'Actually no.
Gally knew M's father well.)

'You leer at her!
'How do you mean, leer?
'Like this, then you spring at her and grab her
'Are you a rugby footballer [. . . ? . . .] X?
'I play for the Metropolitan Police
'Try to imagine that she is an opponent trying to wriggle
through to your goal line.
I don't want to hurt her.
You won't. Girls like that sort of thing.

*

June 25/74

Φ 'Sister' arrives in her car, doesn't go to house, stops
car at gates and goes strolling.
The arrival of 'sister' must be delayed till much nearer
the final sequence. Φ
She must have her scene with Ld E just after she arrives.
Then comes the stuff on June 14, with her walking on
and meeting hero, whom she has met before (How?).
Then she meets Dora and tells her hero's name and the
action starts.
Good X)
Problem: How does she know hero?

Try this. Hero did a portrait of her Peke.

The Peke is with her and barks at Empress and Ld E
curses Peke and 'sister' is v. angry. (*Or* Ld E is afraid
Peke will attack Empress.

Why isn't hero at sty, painting, when 'sister 'comes to sty?
What wd be fine wd be if his delay was due to a scene with heroine.
V. Good)

Try this. Heroine has fixed up all arrangements for eloping. Hero says he can't because he can't let Ld E down and must finish painting Empress before he can leave, and heroine is furious.

(Heroine plans to get out of the house after dinner, and Beach has brought the beverages, by telling Ld E *she wants to see Empress by moonlight*)

XX)

Sequence

1. The quarrel. Φ Heroine breaks engt.

Φ *Hero about to go to sty*)

2. Heroine meets Gally. He comments on her militant air. A girl looked just like that before she stabbed him in leg with a hat pin. She tells him of quarrel. He says it shows how good a heart hero has. Get in the stuff about telling stories of her husband. Heroine won over.

V. Good)

3. G. takes hero back to heroine. Reconciliation. Hero starts for sty.

4. Cut to 'sister' coming to sty. 'Sister' & Ld E

5. 'Sister' & hero.

*

June 25/74

I must get characters and names.

Hero:- Bill Yardley, Freddie Nicholas.

Sister:- Mrs Wentworth MP (Fay). A widow.

Ld Chancellor:- Sir Julius Corder.

Bodyguard:- Sergeant Murchison.

Heroine:- Surname, Garland. Jane Garland. Susan Garland.

Housemaid:- Marilynn.

Lady Garland (Dora). She is a widow.

Try not making hero a professional artist, but painting as a hobby. He should be a schoolmaster or something.

How about a vet? This wd explain his painting animals.
X)
No)

Heroine met him when her dog was ill.

Sir Julius genial. Likes hero.

*

June 26/74

When 'sister' meets Dora, she is v. severe about a shabby
and insolent man she met who was looking after pig.
Dora dismayed says 'That was Clarence'. Any hope
she had had of marrying Ld E to 'sister' died, and
'sister', though not an impressionable woman, had the
feeling that her visit had not begun well. To change an
unpleasant subject she said 'I see you have Mr X staying
here.'

Good)

'He painted my Peke. Your Jane recommended him.'

Sequence

1. Gally and Beach.
2. Gally and Dora.
3. Gally and Heroine. G & Ld E. G. says Ld E must have
   pig painted.
4. Sir Julius and Dora. Bodyguard.
5. Gally and Hero
   Here is a gap to be filled. It should take up 5 and a
   good deal onward.
7. Mrs Wentworth arrives. Scene at sty with Ld E.
8. Mrs W. meets hero.
9. Mrs W and Dora. She tells Dora hero's real name.
7. The quarrel (See June 25)
8. Gally v heroine. He
   **[7, 8 and 9 are ringed; the 7 and 8 following are
   also ringed; and the whole sequence from 1 to the
   second 8 is then crossed out.]**

6. Julius & sister in hotel. [. . . ? . . .]. Dora's invitation has arrived. He tells sister he loves Dora.

7. Hero and Julius in Jno R's taxi. Hero has met Sir J when he came to paint Peke.

1. Beach tells Gally that Dora & heroine are at castle

and Sir J and sister expected. I understand that Sir J will arrive shortly before Mrs W.

X)

*

June 27/74

Ld E & Gally. G. suggests painting pig. Ld E demurs. He reminds G. of the former artists. G says this chap is not like that.

Ld E & Hero. Ld E tells him of former artist who made pig look like drunken pig in Xmas number. Hero reassures him. Ld E criticizes portraits of ancestors. Says his sisters object, but he has got rid of all except Dora.

Good)

and she will be leaving soon. She has brought her daughter here is in love, but she'll get over it soon.

Sequence

1. Sir Julius and sister. He says he loves Dora and is handicapped by bodyguard. He knows Gally. G. coming later.
2. Cut to hero. Gally meets him at station.
3. Ld E & hero.
4. This ought to be hero-heroine. Qy: He tells her he has sold strip in USA.

Sir J-sister.)

Sir Julius met Dora at country house, started to woo her but always bodyguard there. This time he is going to evade him.

*

SCENARIO, Jly 28.

1 to Five, with all the necessary alterations. This introduces Brenda, Sir James, Sergeant Murchison, Dora, Nicky, and mentions Florence. Also plants Lord Emsworth.

Chapter 7 ought to be Gally coming to see hero. Then that part of the story can rest while I get on with Sir James and Dora.

8 therefore, will be the scene between Dora and James in the garden. He has become very sentimental about the old days and is about to propose when Murchison comes up behind him and says it looks like rain and he ought to go indoors. (Here is how I might work the scene. Have TWO interruptions by Murchison. First he comes to warn James about rain. Dora says 'Who is that man? 'My bodyguard'. Then later M comes with macintosh).

9. Now we can cut back to hero. Show him coming out of head-mistress's study. He is in great spirits. He has been sacked because head-mistress has found caricature of herself as Cuthbert the Cat, but he is elated because he has just heard that C the Cat is a success in USA. Butler tells him a gentleman has called to see him. It is Gally. He tells hero he has got him the job of doing portrait of Empress.

10. Arrival of hero at Blandings. Beach lets him in, and he gets idea of Herbert the Hippopotimus. Beach takes him to Florence. Have scene showing hero overawed. Lord Emsworth comes in and relieves hero by being very cordial. Hero gets very fond of Lord E.

11. Hero meets Nicky.

NOTE: This bit from hero's arrival needs a lot of thinking out. I don't want to get to the quarrel scene too soon.

This scenario is only rough, so I will leave it for the moment. The thing to bear in mind is that I MUST get enough stuff between hero's arrival and the quarrel.

There is a gap here.

Everything is foggy till arrival of Brenda.

Try this. At their first meeting Lord E endears himself to hero by being friendly. Then later he takes him into his study to show him photos of Empress and tells him—plug this—that he is his, Ld E's, last chance of getting portrait of Empress. He suggests going to see Emp by moonlight. Coming back, he locks hero out. IF this could lead to something.

*

Aug 8. 1974

Notes for Scenario

Try this. Gally puts jewel in *Florence's* room.

When G. shows it to her, she says 'I don't know how it got there'. 'You think it was what spiritualists call an apport?' 'Brenda wd never believe I stole it: 'Not at first, of course, but gradually the weight of evidence . . . She wd tell the story—dine out on it, in fact—and you wd find people locking up their spoons when ycu were around.'

Gally, before taking F to her room: 'I have been devoting much thought to this case. I bought a copy of What Every Young Detective Ought to Know'.

3. Gally meets Dora. Short scene. 'Where is Florence?' Then play the scene with Florence.

10. Here is where there shd be a passing of time and more stuff before Ld E spills beans. Ld E means to tell F abt Jeff but forgets.

Qy. Ld E makes note in bedside book and discovers it later.
YES)

What I need is some sequence which threatens tc expose Jeff & is averted and reader thinks all is & well then Ld E spills beans.
X)

Query? Have Gally meet Diana after his scene with Vicky.

*

Aug 3. 1974

Notes for Scenario (ctd)

Try this. Plant in 6 that Jeff has given Freddie his cartoon to take to USA.

Then we play arrival of Jeff up to his first scene with Nicky when nothing happens except Jeff & Nicky seeing Dora and James and bodyguard.

Then telegram arrives from Freddie saying he is over in England and is coming to Blandings.

Gally finds Jeff at sty and tells him this. And says he will go to London and explain situation to Freddie and stop him coming.

Gally returns and tells Jeff and N that all is well and that Freddie has sold cartoon and it is success.

Gally goes off to get a drink with Beach.
Gally meets N and she tells him abt quarrel.
He talks her round — this will be just before dressing for dinner.

I don't think I need the locking-out.
Ld E, dressing for dinner, rings for Beach, tells him to send Jeff to him. Jeff arrives and we get the profile and full face stuff. — Jeff.
Meets N. Embraces. Ld E sees them.

Arrival of Brenda must come before this. Show Ld E's dismay at seeing her and lid is put on his [...?...] by Freddie's telegram.
X)

*

Nov 2. 1974

Sequence

1. Sequence ? ? with Ld E seeing Jeff and V embrace and telling Florence that it is Smith whom V loves, not Jeff.

2. F suspects Smith of being Jeff and phones Dame Winkworth and gets a description of Jeff.
3. F tackles Gally Φ who has to come clean. G tells Vicky about F's kicking Jeff out. (This gives V the idea of stealing the jewel). G tells V he will try to egg Ld E to defy Florence. After all, it's his castle.
4. G tells Ld E F wants to kick Jeff out—his last chance of getting Emp's portrait painted. Ld E goes to F and throws his weight about. F has to consent to Jeff staying.

Nov 2. 1974

Sequence

1. Sequence ending with Ld E seeing Jeff. V unhurt and telling Florence how it is a shame when V loves, not Jeff.

2. F suspects Smith; this Jeff and phones Dame Winkworth and gets a description of Jeff.

O.K 3. F tackles Gally, who has to come clean. G tells Vicky that F E kicking Jeff out. (The gives V k idea of stealing the jewel). — G tells V he will try to egg Ld E to defy Florence. After all, it's his castle.

4. G tells Ld E F wants to kick Jeff out — his last chance of getting Emp's portrait painted. Ld E goes to F and throws his weight about. F has to consent to Jeff staying. Is this enough? No. I'll restructure this kicking Jeff —

5. Brenda arrives.

Ld E v F 'It's my castle, isn't it. I'm the Earl of E, aren't I?
'Anything bothering of you all think I'm were a tramp.
'That is a v. offensive remark.
'Join at two holes in your coat.

Φ 3₁ Florence accuses Gally of smuggling
Jeff to castle. G. denies it. F. phones Dame
D for description of Jeff. Having got it, she
Comes back to Gally and accuses him. G. then
tells Vicky.

Then Brenda arrives want say at the time
and Gally straight to Florence's room, leaving
Jewel case in hall.

143

Is this right? **No. F is resolute abt kicking Jeff out. O.K.**)

5. Brenda arrives.

4. Ld E and F 'It's my castle, isn't it. I'm the Earl of E, aren't I?

'Anybody looking at you would think you were a tramp.

'That is a v. offensive remark.

'You've got two holes in your coat.

3. Φ *Florence accuses Gally of bringing Jeff to castle. G. denies it. F. phones Dame D for description of Jeff. Having got it, she goes back to Gally and denounces him. G. then tells Vicky.* **O.K.**)

Then Brenda arrives next day at tea time and goes straight to Florence's room, leaving jewel case in hall.

*

Dec 20/74

Sequence

1. G. tells Ld E Florence is kicking Jeff out.

2. F in hammock. She accuses G. and says she has told V she is kicking Jeff out. G. says she can't because Ld E will not permit it. F caves in.

3. Brenda arrives Δ. B and F. 'I want to show you my jewels'. Beach sent for. Jewel gone.

Δ *P. tells B penniless but wants to marr V. He cd steal your jewel to get money to elope.*)

4. V. tells G she stole jewel to prevent Jeff being kicked out.

He says he will hide it in Ld E's study.

5. Back to B and F. They decide to have Claude search J's room. B suggests this.

6. Φ J catches Claude. J rushes off to curse F. Brave.

7. F tells B abt J being violent. B says that looks as if he were innocent.

Φ *Would it be better if Ld E catches Claude and C explains.*
Ld E rushes off and curses F., who takes offence and says
she's leaving)

'It isn't as if Florence was Connie.

'No, Connie's bite spelled death.

'I'm not afraid of Florence. I once saw her spanked
by her nurse for stealing jam.

Q y Make F divorced and her husband wants reconcilation
She says she is going back to him.
If so, make F more attractive in scene with Jeff.)

Query—Should Gally hide jewel in F's room. Ld E finds
it when looking for stamps. Φ He comes to G in hammock. G. says nobody must know that F is a klepto-
maniac.
Good)

Or looking for something he dropped (Report of Shrop
Agriculture Society) when he was having his row with
F. Finds it behind writing desk.

If F is divorced, make husband Amer. millionaire.
When Gally tells them to elope, he says husband will
give her money. V. says I wrote to him. No answer. G
says the letter must have been intercepted by F.

*

Dec 30. 1974

Sequence

1. F & Gally. F. says Jeff is being kicked out.
2. Gally & Ld E. Ld E furious at this.
X. 2A. G. goes to Ems Arms. Meets husband
3. Brenda arrives. B & F (F. tells abt Jeff and Vicky. B
   goes to her room.
4. Note: Wd it be better to put G. meeting husband
   after B's arrival. G. goes to Ems Arms because he
   has to be alone, to think, which rules out Beach's
   pantry.

145

See next page)
5. Brenda comes to F, says she left jewel case in hall and jewel is gone.

(See next page
6. V tells G she stole jewel. G. takes it and says he will hide it in Ld E's study.
7. F wants J's room searched. B suggests Claude.
8. Ld E goes to J's room, catches Claude.
9. Ld E to F's room. He curses F. Husband pops out and dominates Ld E. Reconciliation.
10. Husband tells Gally. G. asks F. to give V money. F refuses. G to hammock to think.
11. Plus Piper, says he was just going to propose, when M came up with rain coat. G. says Beach has told him M loves maid and says he will keep M away while P proposes.
12. Gally & Murchison. G. back to hammock.
13. Plus Piper. Says he's engaged. Gally gets him to give Jeff architect job. **X painting Piper's portrait.**
14. Gally & Beach. With F gone and Diana marrying Piper and Brenda going (Watch this. Why does B go?) Blandings will soon be all-male again (except for Vicky. Jeff stays on to paint pig.
Note: This is rough, but can easily be polished.

Revised Sequence
1. *F & Gally. F says J is being kicked out.*
2. *Gally goes to Ld E who is furious at F for kicking out his artist and says he is going to tick her off. He does the ticking off off stage and comes back and tells Gally that Jeff is staying on.*
3. *Brenda arrives.*
4. *5 and 6, 7and 8 of former scenario can stand.*
5. *Ld E comes to Brenda and F and curses Brenda (who has told Claude to search J's room). B says she is leaving. F says if B leaves, I leave. They both leave (next day?).*

6. *Gally asks F to give V money. She refuses*
   This takes us to 10 of old scenario, with Gally in hammock
and plus Piper.

2A

P.2. 'F's stepdaughter Victoria. F. married the American millionaire, J. B. Underwood. He died, and she
married a man called Ormsby, who writes plays.

'I met him once. He was with young Duff. ℂ Yes, I
believe they are friends. But I was telling you about
Victoria. Florence most unwisely etc.

Φ It might be better, if Moresby and Claude are
friends, to have Claude not Gally, suggest hiding in
F's suite, which leads up to big scene and reconciliation of F and Moresby.
Brenda just says F and husband are separated. Keep the
vegetarian stuff for Gally's scene with husband at Ems Arms.

*

Jan 9. 1975
Sequence
Φ End on 'distribute it.'

1. F & Gally. F *merely suspects* G of having brought Jeff
   in but can't prove it. Φ Gally's meditations.
2. Brenda arrives. F tells her about suspecting Smith is
   Bennison.
   Brenda advises her to ask Dame Daphne.
   F does this & comes back and tells B she has told
   Vicky that Jeff is leaving. Φ
Φ *or she goes and tells Gally.*)
**[deleted in same red as the two marginal notes
between 3 and 4]**
3. This is B's room. B rings bell and says she is ringing
   for Beach as she left her jewel case in hall. 'There was
   a necklace I wanted to show you'. Beach brings case.

Necklace has gone. (Or B comes to F and tells her abt necklace)

B says she has necklace to show and goes to fetch it & comes back to say it's gone)

They send for Beach to tell him abt 'not leave house'.)

4. Vicky tells Gally she stole necklace. **X** G takes it and says he will put it in Ld E's study. Then follows scenario of Jan 16.

5. Back to F & Brenda. Search Jeff's room.
6. Gally goes to Ld E, says F is getting rid of his artist.

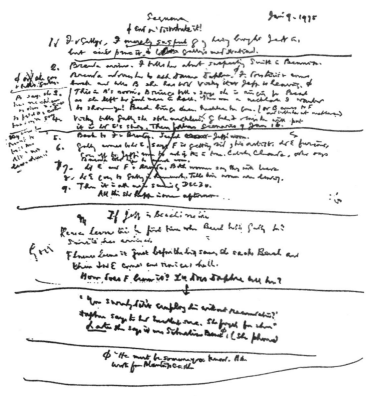

Ld E furious, goes off to Jeff's room to ask if this is true. Catching Claude, who says Brenda told him to search room.

7. Ld E and F & Brenda. Both women say they will leave.
8. Ld E goes to Gally in hammock. Tells him women are leaving.
9. Then it is all as in scenario of Dec 30.

All this shd happen in one afternoon.

[5–9 crossed out]

If Jeff is Beach's nephew
Reader learns this for first time when Beach tells Gally that (?)
Smith has arrived.

Florence learns it just before the big scene. She sacks Beach and then Ld E comes and raises hell.
Good)

How does F learn it? Qy. Does Daphne tell her?

'You surely didn't employ him without recommenda-tion?' Daphne says he had excellent one. She forgets from whom. *Later* she says it was Sebastian Beach Φ. (She phoned)

Φ 'He must be someone you know. He wrote from Blandings Castle.

*

OK)
2) Jan 16/75

Sequence

1. Brenda tells Claude to search Jeff's room.
2. Cut to Ld E and Gally. I want to get them both to Jeff's room. How? Φ
3. Φ Ld E is looking for Jeff. He goes to hammock and asks G if he has seen him. G says 'Perhaps he is in his room'. They go together there, hear crash and go in and find Claude.
4. Claude says Brenda told him search J's room — She

149

thinks he has stolen her necklace. Ld E furious and goes off to tackle Brenda. Gally stays and talks to Claude. Have Gally do the stuff about meek men. Plus Ld E, says he has ticked Brenda off and is now going to tackle Florence. Φ (G must have told him that F. has kicked J out.) They leave, leaving Claude stunned.

Φ *Have stuff about Ld E not being afraid of F. Nothing to Connie.*)

5. They go to F's suite. Brenda is there. F. says Ld E has grossly insulted Brenda, who will leave unless Ld E apologizes. Ld E refuses, and F says she will be leaving this afternoon. Exit Ld E with G. G. praises Ld E.

---

1)

OK to end of page 84. End with F. [. . . musing].
Brenda arrives. F. phones Daphne. Having got the identification, she goes to Gally as written from p. 85 and ending with p. 88. Then as above, starting with Ld E and G going to Jeff's room. (But wait. Gally is agitated. He must tell Ld E Jeff has been fired.

P. 85. F exits.
Gally tells Ld E that Jeff has been fired by F. Ld E furious. I'll tick F. off (Use Connie's bite). They asked Claude. Ld E is even more furious with Brenda, a guest, than with F. He says he is going to find Brenda and give her hell. G says aren't you going to see F? 'Later, when I've crushed Brenda. — Ld E.

*

SCENARIO. Jan 19. 1975
Ch 1. Aziz, with possibly a mention of the bracelet.
Ch 2. Aziz.
Ch 3. Gally and Vicky unchanged.
 In scene between Gally and Florence cut all that about Jeff's father.

F's objection to Jeff is his lack of money. F's husband
is planted [... ? ...]. She tells G he is weak.

Ch 4. Aziz, but can be improved.

Ch 5. Aziz, but Jeff's name ought to be familiar to
Gally.
This is where it should be planted that J's father, the
actor, and Gally were pals.

Ch 6. Aziz, but can be improved.

Ch 7. On page 33 Beach tells Gally Jeff is his nephew.
His brother took the name of Bennison for the stage.
Beach is agitated, Gally calm.
I shall have to think about the uncle-nephew
situation.

Ch 8. Aziz.

Ch 9. Aziz.

Ch 10. Aziz.

Ch 11. Aziz.

Ch 12. Page 67. If Beach is scared of being found out to
be Jeff's uncle, he would not be laughing. Jeff must
hear the rumble of Gally's voice.

Ch 13. Aziz.

Ch 14. Aziz up to end of Page 82.

Ch 15. Aziz to end of Page 84, where Florence must be
left suspecting Gally but realizing that she has no
proof.

ALL THE ABOVE SEEMS STRAIGHT

Ch 16. Brenda arrives. Florence tells her about suspecting Jeff but having no proof. Brenda advises her
to apply to Dame Daphne. She does so and gets
identification. She then goes to Gally and we play
the scene p 86 to 88.

Ch 17. I haven't quite decided on the order in which
events come, but I will put down a tentative sequence.
I think that after leaving Gally Florence go to Brenda
and tell her what has happened. Brenda is distrait.
She says about theft of her necklace, from jewel case

left in hall. '**You can't let this man leave house. He's got my necklace.**'

Ch 18. Vicky tells Gally she stole necklace to prevent Jeff leaving house. Have them consulting Beach as to whether this in only for murder. Gally says he will put necklace in Lord E's study.

Ch 19. Φ **C. Lord consults Beach as to where people in tec stories hide things.** *On top of* [*? wardrobe?*]

SCENARIO.   Jan 19.1975

Ch 1.   Aziz, with possibly a mention of the bracelet.

Ch 2.   Aziz.

Ch 3.   Gally and Vicky unchanged.
In scene between Gally and Florence out all that about Jeff's father.
F's objection to Jeff is his lack of money. But F's husband is ...
... , She left him a week.

Ch 4.   Aziz, but can be improved.

Ch 5.   Aziz, but Jeff's name ought to be familiar to Gally. This is where
it should be planted that J's father, the actor, and Gally were pals.

Ch6.   Aziz, but can be improved.

Ch 7.   On Page 33 Beach tells Gally Jeff is his nephew. His brother took
the name of Bennison for the stage. Beach is agitated, Gally calm.
I shall have to think about the uncle-nephew situation.

Ch 8.   Aziz,

Ch 9.   Aziz.

Ch 10. Aziz.

Ch 11. Aziz.

Ch 12. Page 67. If Beach is scared of being found out to be Jeff's uncle,
he would not be laughing. Jeff must hear the rumble of Gally's voice.

Ch 12. Aziz.

Ch 14. Aziz up to end of Page 82.

Ch 15. Aziz to end of Page 84, where Florence must be left suspecting
Gally but realising that she has no proof.

ALL THE ABOVE SEEMS STRAIGHT

Ch 16. Brenda arrives. Florence tells her about suspecting Jeff but having
no proof. Brenda advises her to apply to Dame Daphne. She does so and
gets identification. She then goes to Gally and we play the scene
p.86 to88.

Ch 17. I haven't quite decided on the order in which events come, but Iwill
put down a tentative sequence. I think that after leaving Gally
Florence go to Brenda and tell her what has happened. Brenda is
distrait. She says about theft of her necklace, from jewel case left
in hall. "You can't let this man leave house. He's got my necklace."

Ch 18. Vicky telss Gally she stole necklace to prevent Jeff leaving house.
Have them consulting Beach as ot whether this is only for murder.
Gally says he will put necklace in Lord E's study.

Continue the scene between Brenda and Florence.
Florence says Jeff must have stolen necklace. They
decide that Jeff's room must be searched. By whom?
Brenda suggests Claude. Claude sent for. Φ
Ch 20. Gally goes to Ld E. Tells him that Florence has
fired Jeff. Ld E furious. Ld E says he will go and see
Jeff and assure him that he won't have to leave.
Where is Jeff? he is probably in his room. 'When you
have a job like painting the Empress, you have to do
a lot of deep thinking.' They go to Jeff's room. As they
reach it, they hear a crash from inside. Ld E thinks
Jeff may have met with an accident. They go in and

Scenario (continued)

Φ C. consults Beach as to how people take things he did. things.
& ways of wording.

Ch19. Continue the scene between Brenda and Florence. Florence says
Jeff must have stolen necklace. They decide that Jeff's room must
be searched. By whom? Brenda suggests Claude. Claude sent for. Φ

Ch 20. Gally goes to Ld E. Tells him that Florence has fired Jeff. Ld E
furious. Ld E says he will go and see Jeff and assure him that
he won't have to leave. Where is Jeff? he is probably in his room.
'When you have a job like painting the Empress, you have to do a
lot of deep thinking.' They go to Jeff's room. As they reach it,
they hear a crash from inside. Ld E thinks Jeff may have met with
an accident. They go in and find Claude. Gally is stern with Claude.
He makes him confess why he is there. He says Brenda told him to
search the room for stolen necklace. L₄ E furious at this slur on
Jeff, rushes off to tackle Brenda. Gally is left to talk to Claude.
Tells him he must expect this sort of thing at Blandings.
Use the stuff about meek men?
Ld E returns, says he has properly ticked Brenda off. And now, he
says, to tick Florence off for firing Jeff. Claude left , stunned.

Ch 21. They go to F's suite, Gally with Ld E to render moral support.
+ X./ + Fr. Brenda is there. (No, I don't think she need be). F. says Ld E
content has grossly insulted Jeff. (Yes, I think the scene wd play
End (I 7 better without Brenda). F says Unless Ld E apologizes, Brenda
Vigin in galun will leave, and if B leaves she, F) will leave. Ld E refuses to
apologize and F says she will leave tomorrow morning.
~~They go away and Gally is pretty bad about same~~. The meek men stuff might fit
They go out together, G praising Ld E. The meek men stuff might
fit in better here.

Ch 22. Gally goes to his hammock. Plus Piper, who says he was just going
to propose when Murchison came up with rain coat, saying the sky
looked threatening. G says Beach has told him that Murch loves maid,
and he will keep him away while Piper proposes.
G goes off to tackle Murch. Succeeds. G es back to hammock.
Plus Piper says he is engaged. G gets him to give Jeff job of
painting his portrait, – and you knoe hundreds of rich people, you
can recommend Jeff to them. P. agrees. *Φ Φ + Ld E with necklace.*
– Ld E.
G sees car draw up at door. Florence comes out and stands wait-
-ing for Brenda. G. goes to her, tells her that Piper has given
Jeff portrait job for princely sum, all his pals in Cabinet will
have their portraits painted by Jeff for princely summ, Ld E will
pay him highly for Empress and Beach will add his bit as a wedding
present. (Bech is J's uncle.? F gtes into car without a word.
End with Gally chatting with Beach.

THE END

153

find Claude. Gally is stern with Claude. He makes him confess why he is there. He says Brenda told him to search the room for stolen necklace. Ld E furious at this slur on Jeff, rushes off to tackle Brenda. Gally is left to talk to Claude. Tells him he must expect this sort of thing at Blandings. Use the stuff about meek men?

Ld E returns, says he has properly ticked Brenda off. And, now, he says, to tick Florence off for firing Jeff. Claude left, stunned.

Ch 21. They go to F's suite, Gally with Ld E to render moral support. Brenda is there. (No, I don't think she need be). F. says Ld E has grossly insulted Brenda. (Yes, I think the scene wd play better without Brenda). F says Unless Ld E apologizes, Brenda will leave, and if B leaves she, F, will leave. Ld E refuses to apologize and F says she will leave tomorrow morning.

+ *X from cupboard. He ticks Ld E off for wanting pig in gallery*)

The meek men stuff might fit. They go out together, G praising Ld E. The meek men stuff might fit in better here.

Ch 22. Gally goes to his hammock. Plus Piper, who says he was just going to propose when Murchison came up with rain coat, saying the sky looked threatening. G says Beach has told him that Murch loves maid, and he will keep him away while Piper proposes.

G goes off to tackle Murch. Succeeds. Goes back to hammock. Plus Piper says he is engaged. G gets him to give Jeff job of painting his portrait,—and you know hundreds of rich people, you can recommend Jeff to them. P agrees. Φ Φ + *Ld E with necklace. — Ld E.*

G sees car draw up at door. Florence comes out and stands waiting for Brenda. G. goes to her, tells her that Piper has given Jeff portrait job for princely sum, all his pals in Cabinet will have their portraits painted by Jeff for princely sum, Ld E will pay him highly for Empress and Beach will add his bit as a wedding present. ? Beach is J's uncle. ? F gets into car without a word.

End with Gally chatting with Beach.

THE END

*

At a very early stage, perhaps back in 1973, Wodehouse felt he had two conflicting novels jostling towards Blandings to be born. In the next sequence of our transcription, which Wodehouse has headed "Novel A" we see the exciting possibility of Bertie Wooster, Jeeves and Stiffy Byng turning up to set the plots at the castle.

*

NOVEL A

Start:– Probably the best account of the fire at X Hall, which is about a mile from Blandings Castle, was in the X, with which is incorporated etc. For some reason the Times, the etc and the other national newspapers did not cover it, but the X did it proud.

Lord E read it while breakfasting. Felt that X, the owner of the Hall, whom he disliked, had been asking for something like this for years.

Lady X tells him they must take X and Co in.

Not using the fire (or possibly using it) try this
1. *Hero and heroine engaged. They have a row. (What about?)*
2. *To keep hero from leaving house, heroine steals necklace. (Whose?)*
3. *Investigations start. Heroine fears she will be found with necklace. (Why?)*

4. *She gives it to someone to hide. (Who? Her brother?)*
See below)
5. *Reconciliation. Heroine asks brother (G) to return necklace. He refuses. (Why? Could make big comic character, Eg a playwright, who wants to keep necklace to finance his play.*
6. *Big comic sequence with hero trying to steal necklace from brother. (How end?)*

Try this. It would be much more plausible if heroine goes to 'brother' and says hero is leaving and she will have no time to get reconciled, and brother **suggests the stealing of necklace and says he will do it.**
Good X)

Then, instead of refusing to return necklace, 'brother' has accident and loses his memory and so we get a situation as in Money In The Bank with brother—uncle?—hero & heroine combining to try to find necklace (This makes 'brother' not crooked, a great improvement).
Good)

Could wife who owns necklace suspect her husband of having stolen it?

*

Novel A

Hero is an artist.
Start with some comic scene with heroine.
She goes with him to his studio.
It is humble and his pictures bad. She thinks he is poor.
Ld E wants pig's portrait. She recommends hero.
Then all the incidents which end in them getting engaged.

*

She says it will be like Bohemian, artistic poverty.
He reveals that he has had a comic strip running in America

156

for years. It has now reached stage where other artists do the drawing.

Good)

Try this. Have a Character (whom Ld E dislikes?) who turns out to be a famous animal painter who is eager to paint Empress.

---

*End. Hero, engaged to heroine, goes to London to buy ring. He meets the man who was engaged to heroine, who has been thinking it over and decided to marry her. Make him very patronizing about her, says he has no doubt she will resume engagement. After all, who is she? (Who **is** she? Parson's daughter? or niece of [?] woman?). Hero says he can see only one objection, that she is going to marry* **him**.

Good)

What Characters have I got?

1. *Hero*
2. *Heroine*
3. *Heroine's fiancé.*
4. *Lord Emsworth*

Only four!

Problems

1. *What does fiancé quarrel with heroine about?*

Ch 1. Hero and heroine meet. They have known each other as kids. 'What are you doing now?' — I'm secty to Lady X at Blandings.

*

Novel A

Try this. Make owner of jewel an important character.(Query. Old flame of Ld E?). Ld E reluctantly in danger of marrying her. Φ

   She finally gets engaged to man who has been staying at 'fire' house, and he turns out to be big animal painter who wants to paint Empress.

This will give me six characters.
Good)
___
Problem. Who is heroine? Φ
___
Φ *Try this. Ld E's sister Dora is at Blandings. She insists on
'fire' lot being taken in and wants Ld E to marry 'jewel'
woman.*
   Heroine is her secretary.
   So now I have seven characters.
Good)
___
*Can I make the man who gets engd to jewel woman the cabinet
minister with detective dogging him. He confides his problem to
Ld E, who does something (like giving tec Mickey Finn which
puts him out of action. He goes off to propose and comes back
and tells Ld E he is engaged.*
*(If I was this, I either scrap idea of big painter and pig or else
have him tell Ld E he knows painter who wants to paint pig.*
Good)
___
*To ask somebody. What does an artist of a successful comic
strip get, and how much when he hands over the strip to other
hack artists?*
___

*

NOVEL A
___

Try it as a Jeeves story.
1. Bertie is staying at Blandings. A niece of Lord Emsworth's
is there, and she and Bertie are great pals.
   Note: Bertie cd propose to her, using that idea of trying to
persuade girl by saying she wd have a husband she cd tell
stories about. And she tells him she is engaged to a man he
knows who lives in the neighbourhood.
2. Girl comes to him in tears and says she has quarrelled with
man and engt broken.
3. Man's house has fire. The inhabitants are asked to stay at
Blandings. Make this plausible. Ld E wd object strongly, so

158

heroine's mother ought to be his sister Dora from Pigs Have Wings, and she over-rules him. So hero comes to Blandings.
4. *Hero has to leave. Then jewel is stolen. (Whose?)*
5. *Heroine comes to Bertie — says she stole jewel to keep hero from leaving house. Lands B with it.*

Good so far but no part yet for Jeeves or Ld E and pig.

I don't believe it's a Jeeves story. I think man heroine loves goes to London, as residents aren't compelled to stay, and run of story is heroine falling for chap she gives jewel to: (This wd make the first man a rotter of some kind.
Work on this)

Heroine steals her mother's jewel. If caught she will get sent to her Grandmother in Bexhill.
X)

Title: Lord Emsworth Entertains.

*

Novel A

If a Blandings story, Bertie goes out at night with Ld E to see pig, Φ who has not been well.

> **Φ Ld E wants him to see pig by moonlight.**

They come back, Ld E in lead. He absent mindedly shuts front door, leaving B locked out.
Good)

B. climbs in through a window and is seen by detective and becomes a suspect (OR climbs in and meets heroine Φ and proposes. She says she is engaged to neighbour.
Φ 'Will you marry me. Not immediately of course. When we have had time to assemble a clergyman or two.)

Try this. Stiffy is at Blandings. Also heroine. Stiffy wants to steal pig ∵ it has become such an obsession with Ld E. (get some stronger motive). Heroine wants to get hero to stay on.

*I don't know if the man afraid of being knighted wd come into
Novel A, but a good solution wd be if some acquaintance of him
and his wife's got made a Lord, and she tells him on no account
to accept a knighthood.*
XX)

<hr>

Sequence

1. Fire. Man comes to Blandings.
2. He & heroine have row.
3. Girl steals jewels, gives them to hero to keep.
4. Hero gives them to Ld E.
5. Man leaves. The company haven't been told to stay.
*6. Hero asks Ld E for the package he gave him. Ld E either has
   forgotten and denies having any package or has lost his
   memory.*
7. Hero searches Ld E's study. Is he caught? By Bertie. Φ

<hr>

Φ *If they both search study, something cd happen eg clap of
thunder, which causes heroine to fall into hero's arms.
(c.f. Uneasy Money).*
This might be good)

*

For six pages of notes (undated, so they may have
been made on six separate days, before the pages dated
December 20th and December 30th) Wodehouse
wondered who this man, 'X' or Kevin, was who was
going, by sudden domination, to earn his return to Lady
Florence's respect and love. Husband? Divorced husband? Fiancé? And/or butler Beach's nephew? we have
transcribed four of these pages.

*

Husband

Clipped moustache. V. military. Appearance misleading, as he was a v. wild man. Very gib and strong.

Vegetarian. F. disapproved. Ridiculous fad! (He has *become* a vegn).

Gally says I was a vegn for a while many years ago because I cd not afford not to be, meat costing so much. (My investments on the turf

Kevin: Dt you think there is any hope of a reconciliation?

Gally: It depends what the row was about. If you have been preferring blondes.

K: Good heavens, no.

G: Then what was the trouble?

K: I became converted to vegetarianism and F called it a ridiculous fad.

G: *You didn't* try to convert *her* to veg.

K: Certainly not.

G tells K to hide in F's suite and jump out at her. Drink G. Ovens beer.

*

Florence's husband

He is Beach's nephew, an actor, or playwright? (need he be B's nephew?)

Gally meets him in Ch. 2. F. has chucked him, if engaged or insisted on a divorce if married, & he has gone to B's pantry for consolation & port. (Gally does not know his father). (Husband is leaving, chucked out)

Problem, why have — call him 'husband' — & F split? Φ And how does their reconciliation affect Jeff?

Φ It looks as if they aren't married. Qy. Shall he have already alienated F? by getting her to put up money to star him if an actor or finance his play, if playwright.

His appearance (1) in Ch 2 (2) At Emsworth Arms after Piper has left & G is alone. (2) In big scene. (In 2 G. has advised him to stoke up on G. Ovens beer)

Φ They are only engaged. Can they have split ∵ she

161

told him to go and make Ld E give up idea of pig in portrait gallery? In big scene he reveals that he has got Ld E to agree to have the pig in study. Φ

Φ I can see good comedy with him reasoning with Ld E,—which wd make F. melt to him.

Husband

Clipped moustache. V. military. Appearance misleading, as he was a v. mild man. Very big & strong.

Vagabonia. F. is it apparent. 'Ridiculous fact'. (He has become a veg.)

Gally says I was a veg for a while many years ago, because I couldn't afford not to be, meant working so much. (My investments on the huff)

Revive, d' you think there is any hope of a reconciliation?
Sally: It depends what the row was about. If you have been preferring blondes
K: Good heavens, no.
F. Then what was the trouble?
K: I became converted to vegetarianism, and I asked it a mistaken fact.
As you told K by to convert her to veg.
K: Certainly not.

G. tells K to hide in F's suite and jump out at her, when G. owns her.

Florence's husband.

He is Rosalie's nephew, an actor, or playwright. (need he be B's nephew?)
Gally meets him in club, & he has clubbed him, & suggests, or insisted on a Titcoue of marriage, or he has gone to his party to consider a book. (Gally does not know his father). (Husband is leaving, Florence out.)

Problem, why have — call his 'husband' & & split? And how does this reconciliation suggest Jeff?
Φ It looks as if they are just married, E.N. Shall he have always absented F by getting her to take up every to some him if an actor or patron in plan, & playwright
His appearances (1) In club (2) At Ownsworth arms after Pilpo has left v F is alone. (3) In big scene, (br 2 F. has advised him to broke up from husband)
Φ if they are only engaged. Can they have split — she told him to go and make L E give up idea of pig in portrait gallery? In big scene he reveals that L E has agreed to pig in study. Φ
Φ I can see good comedy with him reasoning with L E, — which wd make F. melt to him.

X In Ems Arms Scene 'husband' tells S. all abt his quarrel with F.
In G. F moment, says he was weak.
G. and X at Ems Arms. G. advises X to shake up on G's point. Rule.

In Ems Arms scene 'husband' tells G all abt his quarrel with F.

In G-F F merely says he was weak.

X)

G and X at Ems Arms. G advises X to stoke up on G's port & hide.

Big Scene.

Start with Ld E and G entering.

Row. Don't have F saying she will leave. Work up to where F. says something abt pig being in portrait gallery.

X comes out of cupboard.

'I wd like to say a few words on that subject.'

X reasons with Lord E.

Ld E convinced. Goes off to break it to Jeff that his portrait won't be in gallery. He will be disappointed

X and F reconciled.

X says Let's get married and go to USA. Put on my play there.

F says you won't mind V being with us. Can't leave her here with Jeff.

X and F go off, leaving Gally.

Gally muses. Plug snag of Jeff and V being parted.

Enter Piper, wanting smelling salts for Brenda. G. tells what has hapd. G. says abt Ld E furious. Use meek man stuff

Piper complains of Murchison G. offers to get M out of way. Meet me at my hammock if all goes well.

G & Murch. G to hammock + Piper. He is engaged.

G. gets commission for portrait from P.

G. goes off to tell Jeff the news

Qy scene J, V & G. Tells them to elope, they say no money, G says abt commission, & he is going to see Ld E for more.

*

Ch 16

Try this. 1. B arrives. B & F. B says she met 'husband' on train. *Says No.* Begs F to take him back. F says too weak.

No. B is a hard character.
She says Kevin is weak.

(B says he is at E. Arms. B to her room.
2. Cut to Gally, G & Ld E. G. to Ems Arms. Φ G and husband. G advises him to stoke up with G. Ovens ale & hide in F's suite and come out and dominate F.
2 isn't right)
3. B comes to F, report loss of jewel.
4. V. tells G she stole jewel.

(THIS IS RIGHT

Φ G goes to Ems Arms ∴ after his scene with Ld E he goes to hammock and Beach tells him husband rang up fr Ems Arms wanting to speak to Gally.
This makes it all right.)

In 1 F tells B she has to be dominated by her man

2. Qy. Shall I cut architect idea and have Gally tell Piper to have Jeff paint his portrait *as a present to Diana?* Says J is doing excellent job with Empress
Good)

Can I work it so that everything happens in one day?

In Gally's first scene with Ld E, make G's reason for staying in London because he had to console his old pal X. who is F's husband.
V. good X)

For title. Something about women being hard to handle.
Qy. Women are Peculiar.
X)

plate full
grateful

*

In the Preface to his 1929 Blandings novel *Summer Lightning* Wodehouse wrote:

A certain critic—for such men, I regret to say, do exist —made the nasty remark about my last novel that it contained 'all the old Wodehouse characters under different names'. He has probably now been eaten by bears, like the children who made a mock of the prophet Elisha : but if he still survives he will not be able to make a similar charge against *Summer Lightning*. With my superior intelligence, I have outgeneralled the man this time by putting in all the old Wodehouse characters under the same names. Pretty silly it will make him feel, I rather fancy . . .

Seven Blandings novels (eight with *Sunset at Blandings*) and nine short stories came after *Summer Lightning*. One of the difficulties in multi-volumed saga-writing is to know how much introductory explanation you've got to give to an old character in a new novel. When the eighth Blandings novel hits the bookstalls, for how many of its readers will it be their first visit to the castle? And how do you explain Lord Emsworth to these first-time readers without boring your old faithfuls?

Wodehouse dusted away this difficulty in amusing short pieces in the first chapters of several novels. But it remained a difficulty. And, in the later Blandings novels especially, I think that the author found this difficulty getting compounded with others. He came to know his characters so well that he could repeat an introduction that had served him as a repeat in an earlier novel. In the case of *Sunset at Blandings* I am thinking, in passing, of the introduction of Galahad (page 18). This would probably have been re-written, with fresh phrases and rhythms, in a final version, but as it stands it is almost a transcript of the paragraph presenting Gally in *Galahad at Blandings*, which was itself almost a transcript of its equivalent in *Full Moon*.

And Wodehouse knew the Blandings habitat so well by 1974 that he could move his characters like chessmen to and from positions that you feel are almost like chalk-marks on the floor of a stage. In this novel the main moves are to and from the Emsworth Arms, the hammock, Beach's pantry, the croquet lawn, the pig-sty and one or two key bedrooms (always one to be searched for the missing jewel, pig or memoir). In the page of notes dated December 30th 1974 (page 145) Wodehouse wrote 'G. goes to Ems Arms because he has to be alone, to think, which rules out Beach's pantry'. You'd suppose that Gally could have found somewhere in the castle to be alone other than in the pantry—in his own bedroom? practising cannons in the billiard room? having a bath?—without needing to walk three miles to Market Blandings. By the time that this novel would have received its final polish, there would have been a better reason for Gally's move. But at the early note stage it is his need to get away somewhere to think that leads Gally's feet across those miles to the pub.

There is a last difficulty. Wodehouse in his nineties, and, indeed, in his seventies and eighties, was writing short, and sadly conscious that he was writing short. He liked his plots to be as complicated as ever, and he wanted to move his characters in the same mazy notions. But they tended, as he got older, to get from A to B in about a quarter of the number of words that he had so easily given them, straight out of the typewriter, in the three golden decades between 1925 and 1955. In those days, when the scenario was right, the stuff came bubbling out of his mind and pouring into his typewriter. Bertie Wooster would cadge a lunch or submit to some blackmail from his Aunt Dahlia; Lord Emsworth would move from drawing room to pig-sty. And each scene, dialogue or narrative, would be made in a dance of prose well spotted with 'nifties'. At the end of a day he was 2,500 words, good words, to the good. Cutting them down 'raking out the clinker' was a phrase of Kipling's that appealed to Wodehouse, and polishing them to a near-final 1,500 next morning in revision was a pleasurable chore logodaedaly following logorrhea. He met the annual deadline for a novel for the Christmas trade easily, with a stint in Hollywood, work on a couple of plays, and a dozen stories making an average year's output.

In his old age Wodehouse had to start in handwriting: notes, sentences and paragraphs. He couldn't get it going on the machine. And when he totted up the day's score, it might be 500 words, a fifth of what he could do in his *floruit* period. The verbal flourishes and pirouettes just weren't there. They had to be cobbled in later. It was less fun fleshing it out than cutting it down. But he did it. He remained the great provider, with books to size, seamless and without padding. If the going had remained good *Sunset at Blandings* might, under another title, have been ready for Christmas 1976.

*

Well, the revels at Blandings Castle are now ended. But its cloud-capped towers shall not dissolve. And Wodehouse's old brain stayed untroubled to the end. I have not researched this, but my guess is that published novels written by English authors aged ninety-three can be counted on the thumbs of one hand. And if there have been more than that, I would expect to find them tired, petulant, gloomy and grey, showing their author's age; certainly not funny, fresh, young in heart and full of hammocks, sunshine and four pairs of lovers headed for altars in the last pages.

Wodehouse, bless his old heart, went to his honoured grave without issuing a funeral note or a solemn message to anyone, with a farce novel warm in his typewriter. He had earned laurels enough since the 1920s, and, if he had worn them ever, it would have been on the side of his head. He had never rested on them. He went on being frivolous to the last. He had always been very serious about his work of being funny.

THE CASTLE
AND ITS SURROUNDINGS

WODEHOUSE built Blandings Castle from his typewriter and from far away. As a young, struggling, English author in New York, he had been writing, primarily for the American market, light romantic stories set in America. *Something Fresh* (or *Something New*, as it was called in America) justified its name; it was largely farce and it was set in England.

There had been a Shropshire castle, Dreever, in an earlier, but more serious novel, *A Gentleman of Leisure* (November 1910. It had been published in New York as *The Intrusion of Jimmy* in May. And it was later a play, starring Douglas Fairbanks Sr., and, later still, John Barrymore). Dreever Castle had an amorphous Anglo-American house-party, a rose garden, a lake, a butler and a bossy aunt. But it was only a foreshadow of Blandings.

Wodehouse told me that he got the skyline grandeur of Blandings Castle from memories of Corsham Court, near Bath, seen from its frozen lake. He had been taken to skate there by an aunt one winter during school holidays. He had, after leaving the Bank, lived in a small house named Threepwood in the village of Emsworth, on the borders of Hampshire and Sussex and not far from Bosham, and he used those names for his noble family and its title. Owen Dudley Evans, in an appendix to his *P. G. Wodehouse* (1977), suggests that Beatrix Potter's *The Tale of Pigling Bland*, published in 1913, may have given Wodehouse the name for his castle and a succession of later plots. Well, well.

Blandings first opened its gates in 1915. Afterwards,

when Wodehouse was drawn back, story after story, novel after novel, to the green Shropshire pastures, he regretted that he had chosen a location so far from London: about four hours by train. That distance was time-consuming and took a little of the bustle out of his scenarios. The castle drew most of its visitors, genuine and impostors, from London. London was where Lord Emsworth had to go for the opening of Parliament and to hire a new head gardener. Barribault's Hotel, the Drones, Mario's restaurant and secretarial agencies were all in London. And only London provided loony-doctors, detectives and pig-portrait painters. In this story the restless Galahad does the double journey, Blandings/London/Blandings, three times in what seems to be less than a week, but one might suppose that this was his elderly author showing a last defiance of the difficulty with which he had saddled himself in his springtime.

Wodehouse built another stately home of England, Belpher Castle in Hampshire, in *A Damsel in Distress*, published four years after *Something Fresh*. It was very much the same sort of establishment as Blandings, and there are some noticeable echoes of names. And it was within commuting distance of London. It is odd that Wodehouse didn't keep Belpher going and retire Blandings. Well, still not realizing that he had a saga taking shape, he had given the dreamy Earl of Marshmoreton an autumn romance with a charming American chorus girl, and they had married in Chapter 25. For saga requirements Wodehouse needed to have his chatelain a widower. So (this is an informed guess) he closed Belpher Castle and re-opened Blandings to his public. (By that I mean his reading public. But Wodehouse names, once launched, had a friendly way of breeding in space over the Atlantic. When Hollywood, for the second time, made a film of *A Damsel in Distress*, in 1937, one of the songs, written by the Gershwin brothers and recorded in Ira Gershwin's book *Lyrics on Several Occasions*, is given as 'Sung in Totleigh Castle by the Belpher Society for the Preservation of Traditional English Ballads, Madrigals and Rounds'. And another is 'Sung by Fred Astaire to Joan Fontaine on the downs of Totleigh Castle, located in Upper Pelham-Grenville, Wodehouse, England'.)

It was at Blandings Castle that Wodehouse placed the bulk of *Leave it to Psmith* (1923). And, as the stories and novels multiplied, the Blandings pattern remained familiar and always fresh: the hay-harvest weather week after week, the dreamy old widower earl, the bossy sister, the incarcerated niece, the butler, the impostors, the young lovers, the theft, the criss-cross blackmail, the happy endings engineered by fate, or Galahad, or Lord Ickenham.

Wodehouse tells us hardly anything about the past of the castle. It was built of grey stone, solid against possible attack, in the mid-fifteenth century. It had turrets and battlements in profusion. It had interested Viollet-le-duc (1814–1879. French architect, medievalist and writer). It stands at the head of the Vale of Blandings. It is one of the oldest inhabited houses in the country, with fifty-two bedrooms and staterooms, some of which have not been occupied since Queen Elizabeth I and other royalty were visitors. In *Leave it to Psmith* Psmith suggests that Cromwell had been a less welcome visitor. But as Psmith gives the date of Cromwell's visit as 1550, we must suppose either that Psmith wasn't being serious or that it is a misprint that has unaccountably survived.

But now, in the twentieth century, the castle is obviously a very large, comfortable, warm house, set in a great expanse of splendid gardens, with a long curling drive, and with lawns and parkland stretching into sun-soaked distances in all directions. The railway station is Market Blandings. Shrewsbury is over there. You can see the Wrekin from the tower, and the Severn is very much part of the landscape and view. After that we must rely on conjecture, studying the evidences in Wodehouse's texts and piecing together, where we can make them fit, rooms, floors, terraces, gardens, lawns, trees, tennis courts, pigsties, paddocks, streams, water meadows, cowsheds, drives, vistas, villages, churches and railway lines.

But in a succession of Blandings books spanning sixty publishing years you mustn't look for a purist consistency of topography. Not from Wodehouse. You wouldn't say he was careless. Carefree is a better word. He was not disturbed, or even surprised, when devoted readers wrote to him and pointed out that passage A in novel X didn't square with passage B in novel Y. Certainly he has left a large number of difficulties for the jigsaw-puzzler and, I think, four or five positive impossibilities. Yet here we come, offering drawings and maps *in print* — the dust cover of this book, the sketch of Market Blandings station, the end-papers, plans of the ground floor and first-floor interiors of the castle. We have worked them out scrupulously from the Blandings books. But, even if allowances are made (as they must be) for artistic licence, the publishers and I expect to receive a hail of protests, counter-claims and derision for our daring to give fiction the semblance of fact, and staking our claims on probable locations, directions, shapes, sizes and distances in the fabled demesne.

First, artistic licence. Take the sun on the front cover, soon to set behind the hills on the back. Of course the sun wouldn't be setting that way in the northern hemisphere. But the artist has splendidly interpreted his commission, which was to illustrate the title of the book. The magnificence of the castle, the harassed expression of Lord Emsworth, the cool effrontery of Galahad and, in the background, comfort (Beach the butler) and conflict (Lady Florence) — these are fine embellishments. On the back of the book — or left of the whole picture if you have the cover properly framed by now—is the Empress of Blandings in her new sty with, again, Lord Emsworth and Galahad in attendance. You're right. The new sty isn't *there*. You'll find it, correctly placed, we think, on the map that the artist drew from a helicopter and that makes our end-papers (24K*), Ionicus has put the pig and her protectors central to the back cover because they are the central forces for good, Lord Emsworth in all, the Empress in most and Galahad in the best of the Blandings *oeuvre*. You may say that the pivot of this novel is not the pig-sty, but the hammock under the cedars. The artist thought the Empress had a deeper significance in the context of the whole Blandings canon.

Still looking at the cover, you may say the castle ought to be grey, not brown. But remember where that sun is and how the evening light plays tricks with stone colourings. Remember, too, that, with the anxiety about Brenda's lost necklace, with Sir James's inability to propose to Diana, and with Florence and her husband not on speaking terms, a good artist will naturally want to darken the stone and get his brushes thick with sombre symbolism. You may say there ought to be more ivy mantling the frontage of the castle in the cover picture. An agile Jeff could well have climbed what is shown, but possibly on the day the artist painted the cover picture, McAllister had lowered much of the otherwise visible ivy to clear out old birds' nests and mend some of the wiring. Wodehouse did not live to unknot the plot and plotlets of the story inside the covers of the book. It is natural that Ionicus should want to evoke a little of the mood of Childe Roland when he (if it was he; Browning is so obscure) set the slug-horn to his lips.

And, speaking of Childe Roland, what about that tower on the left, with the standard flying from it (17R)?

* These are grid references to the frontispiece map.

On the cover we are looking at the castle from, roughly, the south. Wodehouse refers to that tower in two similar passages in two separate books. It is the tower over the west wing of the castle, and it is separated from the main block by a gravel path. It seems to be served by a small, dark door at ground level and inside, winding steps to the roof. It is a footman's duty to run the flag up in the morning and lower it in the evening, apparently taking it away with him and locking the ground-level door for the night.

It was on the turret of this tower that Lord Emsworth looked forth through his telescope and saw his son Frederick kissing Aggie Donaldson in the water-meadows by the lake ('The Custody of the Pumpkin', *Blandings Castle*). It was twenty-seven times round its chimney stack that Monty Bodkin had seen Galahad chase his nephew Ronnie with a whangee for having put tin-tacks in his chair. It was here that Sue Brown, sighing her soul for the blows that fate was dealing to her engagement to Ronnie, was unobserved by the flag-lowering footman and was locked up, or in, till jealous Ronnie came to rescue her and found Monty's tell-tale hat (*Heavy Weather*).

What was this tower, other than a pedestal for the flag-pole? What and where was the west wing if this solitary tower dominated it? This is a crux. We have tackled it boldly. We have made the tower dominate a west wing *which is no longer there*. It has all gone to ruin, and its battlements, halls and dungeons have given their stone to the more modern parts of the estate. The curtain wall, what's left of it, guards nothing now, and gardens, lawns and meadows cover the courts where Threepwood after early Threepwood jousted, sang madrigals, gloried and drank deep.

Then, in the early nineteenth century, the sixth earl's factor got that Shrewsbury architect (name unknown) to re-plan the patched-up old fortress as a comfortable manor house, with Georgian grace, primitive central heating in addition to the huge open fires, double-hung sash windows, bathrooms and lavatories plumbed in and the facilities for getting the food hot from kitchens to tables. But the west wing remained as a name only, its last remaining reality being the singular tower flying the Emsworth flag. Or that's the way we read it.

And, though there is no record of Lancelot ('Capability') Brown re-shaping the park, our guess is that the fourth earl had met Brown when he was at work on Weston Park, near Shifnal, for Lady Wilbraham, and got him to make Blandings, from boundary to boundary, his next commission. Give them twenty-five years to settle and mature — much longer for young cedars — and those vistas, those clumps of Scotch firs ('Brown's buttons'), those free-roaming gardens . . . they would grow in grace, beyond fashion, and be vulnerable only to a profligate heir (one has to worry about the present Lord Bosham, what little one knows of him) and alien property developers.

Vanessa Polk, in *A Pelican at Blandings*, looked from the tower and could see the Wrekin (12A) and 'a fascinating panorama of Shropshire and its adjoining counties'. She must have been looking north to north-east. And she would have been able to see the tributary of the Severn (13D) that watered Market Blandings and flowed below the garden of the Emsworth Arms. But the Severn itself was also distantly visible if you looked south across the lake (*Leave it to Psmith, Summer Lightning* and *Heavy Weather*). So Blandings Castle is lapped in one of Sabrina's fair curves. Our end-papers show you how. Don't compare them too closely with any of those misleading county maps.

If you had asked Wodehouse how, exactly, he had seen the rooms, the gardens, the trees, the woods and the landscapes in his mind, he would have shuffled his feet modestly and changed the subject in order to prevent himself from replying, testily, that he couldn't be bothered with details unless they affected his immediate plot and scenario. He could give Lord Emsworth five sisters or ten. He could put a Gutenberg Bible in the Museum (*Something Fresh*) and then, in all subsequent books, forget both the museum and its bible.* He could put the Amber Drawing Room upstairs in one book and on the ground floor (with french windows) in others. He could magic a deserted gamekeeper's cottage into the West Wood (6S) just when he needed it and without the son of the house (Freddie) knowing even of its existence. He could have Lord Emsworth looking out of the Library window and seeing Baxter going in at the front door (*Summer Lightning*). He could have the evening sunlight shining on Baxter's spectacles when he was outside the window of the Writing Room ('The Crime Wave at Blandings'). Accept that since so many rooms, in so many contexts, are described as looking out onto the terrace, the terrace must go round three sides of the house. Those last two data confound our positioning of the Library and the Writing Room. And it is a wrench, for me, to have Baxter (always making difficulties, this Baxter) pelting flower pots into Lord Emsworth's bedroom (*Leave it to Psmith*) from the eastern terrace. But we will accept objections only from such critics as can make composite maps that elucidate more of the clues overall than ours do.

We have made a brave start. It is up to others, now, to find a more workable plan for rooms, terraces and Shropshire sunshine. Wodehouse has left it to us, his followers and fans, to map it all out if we wish and as we

* Blandings has achieved its own fictional immortality. It has also, in a small but delightful way, made a factual footnote in the scholarship of rare books. In *Something Fresh*, you may remember, Lord Emsworth's Museum occupied a room off the great hall:

'The place was simply an amateur junk-shop. Side by side with a wish, and to make it work as close to his clues as possible. Where it does work, it works like a charm. Where it doesn't, it's artistic licence on his side and a problem on ours, to be settled as best suits the probabilities. That Amber Drawing Room, for example. It was first mentioned in the short story 'The Go-Getter', first published in 1931, and it was specified as having french windows. After the great dog-fight, the Rev. Beefy Bingham's Bottles v. Lady Alcester's airedale, Beefy had 'thrown Bottles out of the window' — a thing he would never have done, even to someone else's dog, if the room had been upstairs. But in *Galahad at Blandings* Huxley Winkworth and Lord Emsworth, separately, sneaked away from tea in the Amber Drawing Room and went *downstairs* to the hall and the open air. In *A Pelican at Blandings* (1969),

---

Gutenberg Bible for which rival collectors would have bidden without a limit, you would come upon a bullet from the field of Waterloo, one of a consignment of ten thousand shipped there for the use of tourists by a Birmingham firm . . .'
The Museum hasn't lasted, but its Gutenberg Bible has had a curious after-life. In his 'Occasional Publication' monograph, *One Hundred Books in College Library* (1970), Sir Robert Birley, quondam Head Master of Eton, writes of the near-perfect copy of the Gutenberg Bible presented to Eton by John Fuller, the last Member of Parliament to be imprisoned by the House of Commons for defying the Speaker. (Fuller died in 1831.) There are only forty-eight known copies of this, the first printed book, in the world, though there have been rumours of a recent find in a church in Germany. Forty-eight was the number at the time when Sir Robert wrote his monograph. Sir Robert added to his note on the Eton copy 'To the recorded copies of the Gutenberg Bible should be added one in the library of Blandings Castle in Shropshire.' Within weeks of the publication of *One Hundred Books in College Library*, the Eton Librarian received a letter from the keeper of the rare books section of the Library of Congress in Washington asking for full particulars of this copy of the Gutenberg and the whereabouts of Blandings Castle. The Librarian told Sir Robert about this enquiry and Sir Robert was happy to be able to pass on the good news to Wodehouse.

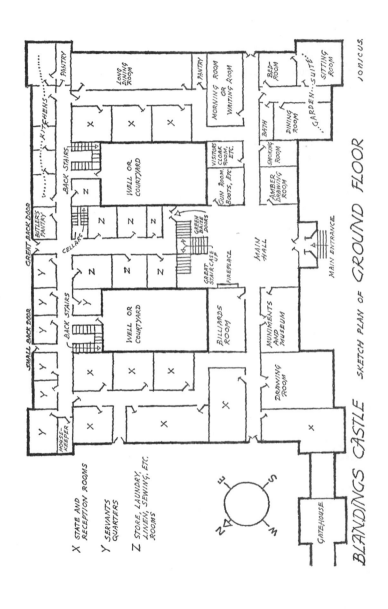

BLANDINGS CASTLE   SKETCH PLAN OF GROUND FLOOR

IONICUS.

X STATE AND
   RECEPTION ROOMS

Y SERVANTS
   QUARTERS

Z STORE, LAUNDRY,
   LINEN, SEWING, ETC.
   ROOMS

the Amber Drawing Room is safely back on the ground floor, and that's where we have placed it. There is another drawing-room on the first floor. There may be more than one. It was out of an upstairs drawing-room window that Connie Keeble's necklace dropped to Eve's feet on the terrace in *Leave it to Psmith*.

The Empress of Blandings is twice brought (or pushed or pulled) into the castle. The first time (*Uncle Fred in the Springtime*) she goes through french windows into the Garden Suite, to be lodged in the bathroom there. So the Garden Suite is on the ground floor. The Duke of Dunstable is its resident guest. The second time that the Empress makes her entrance, in *Full Moon*, Galahad is in the Garden Suite and she goes in at the french windows again and—quite a long journey as pigs go—up the main stairs to Veronica's bedroom, the Red Room. Wodehouse says there that the Red Room is 'on the second floor', which is American for 'first floor' (the floor above the ground floor). When the Duke of Dunstable is in the Garden Suite we are told that the morning sunlight shines into his bedroom. These are the sorts of snippets of evidence on which our artist has worked.

Morning sun comes from the east, so the Garden Suite is situated that end of the castle. And it is 'on the right side of a passage going off the hall'. It is confusing that, though there is a Blue Room bedroom upstairs, the bedroom of the Garden Suite is called the Blue Room. And there is a bedroom upstairs called the Garden Room.

The Picture Gallery and Portrait Gallery are a problem too. In *Heavy Weather* there is a space upstairs referred to as 'the combination drawing-room and picture gallery in which Blandings Castle was wont to assemble before the evening meal'. But a mere fifteen pages later Lady Julia steps out of this room through its french windows to cool off on the terrace. Surely the great hall of the castle rises at least two floors to its ceiling, if not higher, to a skylight in the roof. We have put the Picture Gallery on the first floor, round the well of the hall. There are certainly portraits elsewhere than in this gallery. When Lord Emsworth, in *Something Fresh*, comes down the stairs and fires six shots from his revolver into the hall, his sixth shot hits a life-size picture of his maternal grandmother in the face (which looks like George Robey's) and improves it out of all knowledge. That portrait must have been hanging in the hall. It is possible that there are two galleries, as we have them, the picture gallery *and* the portrait gallery. In which, then, did the Duke of Dunstable hang his nude in *A Pelican at Blandings*? There is no doubt that it was upstairs. In which gallery would the portrait of the Empress be now if his sisters have not forced Lord Emsworth to keep it to himself in his study?

We confess to uneasiness about the design of the stairway down into the hall. Does it go straight up to the first-floor Portrait Gallery, or, as our artist has limned it, right and left at a half-landing? If we are wrong, and if it is the former, it makes much better sense of that cascade of bodies, the Duke of Dunstable's and Johnny Halliday's, in *Galahad at Blandings*. Halliday had been pushed on the first-floor landing by the mysterious (and largely unexplained) Howard Chesney, and he had fallen onto the Duke in front of him, so that they had both crashed down the slippery slope. It was a rather desperate ploy to get (a) the Duke bedroom-bound with a twisted ankle, threatening to sue his host and (b) Halliday rendered unconscious. Not for the first time in a Wodehouse story is a hero rendered unconscious so that the angry heroine shall suddenly come over all motherly, forgive him his sins and kiss him better. Here Linda Gilpin, hitherto furious that her beloved Johnny had, as a barrister doing his duty by his client, torn her, and her testimony, to pieces in the witness box and made her look a prize fool,

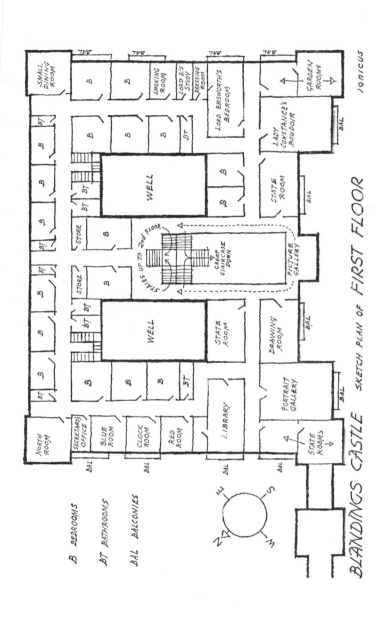

BLANDINGS CASTLE — SKETCH PLAN of FIRST FLOOR

IONICUS

B BEDROOMS
BT BATHROOMS
BAL BALCONIES

SMALL DINING ROOM
B
B
SMOKING ROOM
LORD E'S STUDY
DRESSING ROOM
LORD EMSWORTH'S BEDROOM
GARDEN ROOMS
LADY CONSTANCE'S BOUDOIR
BAL

BT
B
B
B
B
B
DT
WELL
B
B
STATE ROOM
BAL

BT
B
B
B
BT
STORE
B
STAIRS UP TO 2nd FLOOR
GREAT STAIRCASE DOWN
PICTURE GALLERY

BT
B
B
STORE
B
WELL
STATE ROOM
DRAWING ROOM
BAL

BT
B
B
B
B
BT
LIBRARY
PORTRAIT GALLERY
BAL

NORTH ROOM
SECRETARY'S OFFICE
BLUE ROOM
CLOCK ROOM
RED ROOM
STATE ROOMS
BAL

BAL
BAL
BAL
BAL

sees him unconscious and is soon showering kisses on his upturned, though senseless, face.

It would have been difficult, if not impossible, for the Duke and Johnny Halliday to have bounced together over a half-landing and continued their precipitation into the hall. But can you position the pillar in the gallery near which the efficient Baxter kept his nightly watch (*Something Fresh*) if the stairs are a single plane from hall to gallery? If we have got it wrong, perhaps under a single-plane stairway is the recess where the telephone extension is and where Lord Emsworth keeps the hats that he doesn't want his sisters to give away to jumble sales.

The two ultimate challenges to our path-finding abilities inside the castle and out are in the story 'The Crime Wave at Blandings' (*Lord Emsworth and Others*) and in the novel *Pigs Have Wings*. In 'The Crime Wave' from what windows, at what ranges, with what type of airgun were those shots fired at Rupert Baxter those several times? And where exactly was Baxter (a) when picking up that cigarette end and (b) when astride his motor-bike? And where was Beach the butler when Constance Keeble missed a sitter in his direction? Where was the shrubbery in which Jane was crying her eyes out when she saw Lord Emsworth take his shot from the Library window? Where was the seat on which Baxter was sitting when he heard the confession to the crime? Some of your shrubberies and terraces, and the seat itself, must be imagined, we think, behind walls that cut off the view — for instance, the shrubbery in which Jane was crying must have been behind that ruined curtain wall of the old keep, just west of the solitary West Tower (17R).

And, next test: from *Pigs Have Wings* plot on the map, ours or your own, the hitherings and thitherings in the thefts and counter-thefts of pigs between their own sties, alien sties, Sunnybrae and shrubberies. That's a real twister.

On our own map, the cottage (29N) in what is probably called the East Wood is where McAllister, the head gardener, lives and where Aggie Donaldson was staying when she ensnared the heart of lucky young Freddie. You can bet that in his little patch of home garden McAllister grows prize hollyhocks and roses at Lord Emsworth in the way those two Norfolk squires, Lord Bromborough and Sir Preston Potter, Bart., grew moustaches at each other in the Mulliner story 'Buried Treasure'. It was in those water-meadows (15Y) that Lord Emsworth spotted Freddie and Aggie canoodling. It was in the park under those trees (23, 24U) that, in *Service with a Smile*, the Church lads pitched their tents and George, Lord Emsworth's grandson, photographed grandpa cutting the little perishers' guy ropes at dawn. It was thereabouts, too, that the tenants came for the Bank Holiday binge ('Lord Emsworth and the Girl-Friend' in *Blandings Castle*). The tea-tent, in which Lord Emsworth's top hat was sent flying by a crusty roll and his stiff collar wilted, was pitched there, too, to achieve furnace heat under the blazing afternoon sun.

It was to that bathing hut, which Galahad calls 'bath house' (19U), that the Rev. 'Beefy' Bingham dragged the unconscious ninth earl out of the lake. Under the alias of 'Popjoy' (the usual reason—to be near the girl he loved, who had been brought to the castle to keep her away from him) he had surprised his host while bathing. Lord Emsworth had gone for an early morning swim to cool his throbbing ankle, twisted in a fall caused by this clumsy 'Popjoy' man. 'Popjoy' had recommended an embrocation for the ankle, and it proved to be a liniment for horses, not humans. Result: a night of agony and a dawn trip to the lake. So cooling and therapeutic to the ankle were its waters that Lord Emsworth in mid-lake started singing for happiness. 'Popjoy' heard him, thought he was drowning and calling for help, and plunged in to his rescue. To prevent Lord Emsworth struggling, 'Beefy'/'Popjoy' knocked him out with a blow to the jaw as prescribed in all life-saving manuals, and dragged him to shore. ('Company for Gertrude' in *Blandings Castle*). The Rev. R. Bingham's vicarage must be just behind the church at Much Matchingham (27G) and his wife Gertrude is within easy call of her cousin Jane Abercrombie ('The Crime Wave at Blandings' in *Lord Emsworth and Others*) in the factor's house (25M). And if old Belford is still rector of Market Blandings (22B) then, when his son and daughter-in-law Angela ('Pig-Hoo-o-o-o-ey!' in *Blandings Castle*) are staying with him, that makes three Threepwood nieces, cousins and ex-prisoners of the castle, now neighbours.

If you can't quite see the hammock for which Galahad and his sister Florence compete in this novel, it's hidden between the two cedars (25R). It's a long earshot to the stables and garages whence, in *A Pelican at Blandings*, Galahad could hear the harmonica-playing of Voules the chauffeur. But perhaps Voules was a noisy executant and probably he had the breeze behind him. You can see the pond in the kitchen garden (23N) which apparently Galahad as a boy couldn't. He fell into it and, according to one of his sisters, the pity of it was that he was ever pulled out by that gardener. Beyond (24K), is the Empress's new sty, within squeal of the cottage of her caretaker and caterer (26L). And you will notice that, in the paddock where she is housed, there are two other fatties, white this time. It has long saddened us that Wodehouse, beyond mentioning piggeries once (in the plural), never specified that the Empress had any companionship of her own kind. Our sentimental artist has added a couple and thus trebled the pig-man's work for him.

There were deer in the park in the two earliest Blandings books. But we think that the problems of fencing, ha-has, winter feeding and (whisper it) poaching decided Lord Emsworth to let the herd (Japanese and Sika) run down, and to give the remainder to a not-too-neighbourly landowner he met at one of those Loyal Sons of Shropshire dinners. It was quite a business rounding the deer up and carting them. Shropshire has wild deer these days the way East Anglia has coypus, and direct descendants of escapees from the Blandings herds are sometimes seen in the West and East Woods and in the copse north of the stables (14N). Nobody molests them, though McAllister would like to. He curses them when they get into his gardens, and the foresters don't like the way they eat the bark off young trees.

In *Heavy Weather*, at the end of Chapter 6, we read: 'Sir Gregory Parsloe hurried from the room, baying on the scent like one of his own hounds'. Can this mean anything but that Sir Gregory is the local Master of Foxhounds? Whether or no, Lord Emsworth has the living of Much Matchingham in his gift (end of 'Company for Gertrude' in *Blandings Castle*). Is it conceivable that Matchingham Hall is on the Blandings estate and that the hated Sir Gregory, M.F.H., is one of Lord Emsworth's tenants, but claiming the right to hunt his landlord's land? There is mercifully little about blood sports in the Blandings books, though we know Gally kept his gun at the castle (*Summer Lightning*), Lord Emsworth has a pistol with ammunition (*Something Fresh*) and Colonel Wedge comes to the castle with his service revolver ready for use (*Full Moon*). Add to these young George and his airgun, and it still doesn't make a bloodthirsty household.

You can see horses in that paddock (7U). I doubt if they are hunters. There is better evidence for them than for the supernumerary pigs. Hugo Carmody rode, in his secretarial days at the castle (*Summer Lightning*). You see cows in a far field (16, 17K). Those provide milk for the castle and would sometimes, when their grazing is changed, use the cow-byre (10V) where, on the afternoon of the Bank Holiday binge, Lord Emsworth found his little slum-child girl friend. And you can see (5P) the house in Blandings Parva, with the garden at the front, where that girl had quelled the aggressive dog, and brother Ern had bitten Constance in the leg. Just where the girl was when she copped McAllister with a stone is not utterly clear.

Where are the boundaries of Blandings set? Of what noble species are those huge ducks on the Blandings Parva pond (1Q)? Under which of the gravestones in Blandings Parva churchyard (2N) are Lord Emsworth's parents, and his late wife for that matter, buried? We assume that it is to Blandings Parva that they went to church (the only such occasion specified) in *Something Fresh*, though then they had staying in the house party one bishop and several of the minor clergy. Who is living at Sunnybrae cottage (6G) now? Galahad put one of his Pelican Club friends into it, but the man got scared of the country noises and went back to London. Into which window of the castle does Jeff climb in this book, to meet the startled Claude Duff? Where is the little dell near the small spinney in which Baxter's parked caravan invited pig-stealers plus pig (*Summer Lightning*)? Who has left that gate open (18L)? And are those (2G) boys from Shrewsbury sculling for home?

These are good questions. Where we have tried to answer others, we claim no originality of interpretations. What we do claim is that we have done a good deal of homework. Whether we have got the answers which would have pleased Teacher, we can never know, since he is no longer at his desk.

THE TRAINS
BETWEEN PADDINGTON
AND MARKET BLANDINGS

FROM my earliest readings in Wodehouse I had had a
suspicious eye on the trains that connected Paddington
and Market Blandings. I thought the author was inventing
train-times as the mood took him, hardly looking back to
earlier chapters of a book, let alone to earlier books. I
doubted whether any of his train-times would square with
the *Bradshaws* or *ABC*s of the publication dates of the
books in which they occurred.

Not that I would hold it against him if that's the way
he was doing it. But I wanted to see, and particularly to
see if train-times provided any evidence of where in
Shropshire Blandings Castle might be. There are, or
there were in the days of the 1953 *Encyclopaedia Britannica*
(Sarsaparilla to Sorcery), 1,346.6 square miles of Shropshire. Perhaps the railway evidence in the books might
help us to put the mythical Blandings on a real map.

No scholar, as far as I know, had collected all the railway references and laid them out for inspection. So, since

this last chronicle of Blandings adds one last train to the time-table, I have brought them all together. It was not difficult, only laborious. But interpreting the references was beyond me. I could see no pattern, if any existed, in the times and speeds. I could see one obvious anomaly. In *Leave it to Psmith,* Psmith says it's roughly a four-hour journey either way. But, elsewhere in the same book, the narrative says that the 1250 from Paddington arrived at Market Blandings 'about 3 o'clock' (1500). My guess is now that that '3' was originally a misprint for '5' and has persisted uncorrected through half a century of editions. Otherwise we have a train, not even called an express, doing the four-hour journey in 2 hours 10 minutes.

Besides, as recently as 1969, when Wodehouse was eighty-seven, he said to Peter Lewis of the *Daily Mail,* at the end of an interview at his Long Island home, 'By the way, about how long does it take now from Paddington to Shropshire? About four hours? Good, I always made it about four hours.

To avoid the bother of a.m. and p.m., I have translated all train times to the Continental clock. And I have added the publication dates of the books from which I combed my references. It looked professional and it might provide clues. And I have included the 'stops at —' and 'first stop —' details as given in the texts. We get them only four times, always on trains from Paddington. And in three cases out of the four they have a purpose.

I can see no point in Freddie Threepwood adding 'first stop Swindon' in relating to Bill Lister that the girl of his (Bill's) heart has been sent to Blandings on the 1242 (*Full Moon*). But with the 1615 express, the addition of 'first stop Swindon' in *Something Fresh* is a plant. Ashe Marson and Joan Valentine are travelling to Blandings together, he to be valet to an American millionaire, she to be lady's maid to the millionaire's daughter. There is a little job of retrieving for the millionaire the priceless scarab that

Lord Emsworth has forgetfully pocketed and then assumed to be a most generous gift. And the millionaire will pay handsomely for it to be returned for him. Since both Ashe and Joan are out for the reward, Joan wouldn't mind if Ashe were eliminated from competing. So, between Paddington and 'first stop Swindon', she tells him grisly tales of the hardships and snubs that lesser servants have to suffer below stairs. Having frightened him, she says 'Wouldn't you now like to get off at Swindon and go home?'

And when, in 'Pig Hoo-o-o-o-ey!' in *Blandings Castle*, the 1400, 'best train of the day', stops at Swindon, it is with a jolt just sufficient to wake Lord Emsworth up and make him realize that he has already forgotten the master hog-call that might make his beloved Empress start eating again.

The third purposeful stop is the 'first stop Oxford' for the 1445 express in *Uncle Fred in the Springtime*. Lord Ickenham, king of impostors, is gaily travelling towards Blandings Castle in the guise of Sir Roderick Glossop, the loony-doctor. With him is Polly Pott, in the guise of his secretary. And his quaking nephew Pongo is with them in the guise of Sir Roderick's nephew. So far, so snug in a first-class compartment. But then the Efficient Baxter is seen getting into the train at Paddington, and he starts by being suspicious of the whole party. But worse, much worse, is to come just as the train is pulling out. The real Sir Roderick himself gets on. This really is a facer for Uncle Fred. Lord Emsworth had told him that, pursuant to his sister's commands (it was she who was worried about the Duke of Dunstable being potty), he had gone to London to make the acquaintance of the great alienist and persuade him to come to Blandings to vet the Duke. But, Lord Emsworth said, he had discovered that Sir Roderick was the grown-up version of the horrid little boy they had called 'Pimples' at school. Sir Roderick, thus addressed by Lord Emsworth today, had refused the invitation to Blandings. That then enabled Lord Ickenham to set up his three aliases and his triple storming of the castle: on Lord Emsworth's behalf, and to help a couple of young couples find happiness. 'Help is what I like to be of,' says Lord Ickenham.

And here was Sir Roderick Glossop, in person, getting on to the train at Paddington, having changed his mind. Lord Ickenham needed that stop at Oxford badly. It gave him time to talk Sir Roderick into believing that the patient he had been so hurriedly sent for to inspect had turned the corner and needed no immediate attention: so Sir Roderick could go back to his busy practice, stepping off at Oxford and catching whoknowswhat train home to London.

Finally, if train times helped to give Market Blandings a position on the map of Shropshire, we might decide which way the Vale of Blandings went. We put the castle at the end. For how many miles does the Vale stretch? Is Market Blandings short of, or beyond Shrewsbury, its nearest reasonable-sized shopping town? Do you turn left or right for Shrewsbury when you come out of the castle drive on to the main road?

I decided to ask the help of a friend of mine who had been a *Bradshaw* expert at his (and my) preparatory school, long before he joined British Railways as a career. This was the evidence I supplied:

Trains from Paddington to Market Blandings

0830 express (*Sunset at Blandings* 1977). The train that arrives at 1610 (*Service with a Smile* 1961).

1118 (*A Pelican at Blandings* 1969).

1145 (*Service with a Smile* 1961).

1242 'first stop Swindon' arrives 'shortly before 1700' (*Full Moon* 1947).

1250   arrives about 1500—i.e. about 2 hours 10 minutes ? this a misprint *(Leave it to Psmith* 1923).

1400   'best train of the day'. Stops at Swindon *(Blandings Castle* 1935).

1423   *(A Pelican at Blandings* 1969).

1445   express. First stop Oxford (*Uncle Fred in the Springtime* 1939).

1515   *(Blandings Castle* 1935).

1615   express. Stops at Swindon *(Something Fresh* 1915). An express that arrives c. 2105. Restaurant car (*Leave it to Psmith* 1923 and *Uncle Fred in the Springtime* 1939).

1705   'there is nothing between the 1400 and this' *(Blandings Castle* 1935).

Trains from Market Blandings to Paddington

0820   'arrives about noon' (*Uncle Fred in the Springtime* 1939).

0825   (*Uncle Fred in the Springtime* 1939).

0850   arrives about midday (*Leave it to Psmith* 1923).

1035   *(Service with a Smile* 1961).

1050   *(Something Fresh* 1915).

1115   *(Hot Water* 1932).

1240   arrives shortly before 1700 *(Full Moon* 1947).

1400   *(Blandings Castle* 1935 and *Uncle Fred in the Springtime* 1939).

1445   *(Heavy Weather* 1933 and *Uncle Fred in the Springtime* 1939). 'the afternoon train' *(Something Fresh* 1915).

1445   Car at the Castle at 1400 sharp (*Leave it to Psmith* 1923).

1800   *(Full Moon* 1947).

Notes:

1. There are also branch-line trains mentioned. Bridgeford (can this mean Bridgnorth?) to Market Blandings

takes 30 minutes (*Leave it to Psmith* 1923). A train leaves Market Blandings towards Norfolk at 1240, and there's one that returns from the Norfolk direction at about 1945 'in time to dress for dinner' (*Heavy Weather* 1933).

2. Blandings Castle is in Shropshire. The Severn flows through its grounds. Shrewsbury is 45 minutes by car, not hurrying. Market Blandings is 2½/3 miles from the castle (that includes ¾ miles of the castle drive). You can see the Wrekin from the battlements of the castle. [P.S. I ought not to have assumed that the Severn flowed through the castle grounds. What it says in *Leave it to Psmith* (1923) is: 'Away in the distance wooded hills ran down to where the Severn gleamed like an unsheathed sword: up from the river rolling parkland . . .' Whose parkland? Probably Lord Emsworth's, but, if so, perhaps the Severn marks his boundary there. My assumption gave some trouble.]

My expert friend passed on my evidences to a friend of his, Colonel Michael Cobb, who, besides knowing his *Bradshaw*, had the extra advantage of specializing in surveying during an army career in which he spent a number of years on the Ordnance Survey. Colonel Cobb produced a most learned report.

COLONEL COBB'S REPORT

From an initial glance at the problem it is clear that there are railway inconsistencies, such as Blandings Castle being on the Severn and in Shropshire, and yet one could get a train to its station from Paddington with a 'first stop at Swindon'.

I realized that I must discard certain data. I have tried to find a place which fits the main topographical data and which lies within the limits of the largest number of the railway facts.

The topographical data are as follows: the castle is in
Shropshire; the Severn runs through its grounds; it is 45
minutes by car to Shrewsbury, not hurrying; the Wrekin
is visible from its battlements; it is 2½ miles or so from the
castle to its station.

These data limit one to the environs of the Severn
between Bridgnorth and Ironbridge, between Nesscliff
and the Welsh border, possibly to Baschurch. (N.B.
Oldswood Halt station was opened only in the middle-to-
late 1930s.)

I took one railway fact—that it is generally a 4-hour
journey from Paddington (1923), and a fast train takes
about 3 hours 40 minutes (1947). I applied this to the
above three areas. *Bradshaw* shows that the through trains
only stop at Wellington (under 3 hours from Paddington)
and, excluding Shrewsbury itself, Gobowen (about 3
hours 40 minutes). This latter puts Blandings Castle
eight miles from the Severn, which means that the river
could hardly flow 'through its grounds' (though it might
flow through its land, but that is not the same thing). It
also puts the castle in the suburbs of Oswestry. This is so
unlikely that I discarded Gobowen.

At this stage I decided that there must be a change of
trains for the passenger from Paddington to Market
Blandings. This opens up:

1. The Shropshire and Montgomeryshire Railway, which
   was a possibility between Nesscliff and Kinnerley
   Junction. But the trains were sparse and I feel sure that
   Wodehouse would have referred to their quaintness at
   some stage.
2. The main-line intermediate stations between Wellington and Shrewsbury, such as Walcot and Upton
   Magna, and the one possibly north of Shrewsbury,
   Baschurch. These all put the castle in the right
   topographical position. But I found that the local

193

services were too sparse to give Wodehouse the
frequencies he required.
3. The Severn Valley line. Here one could only just reach
Bridgnorth in 3 hours 40 minutes from Paddington by
one train, and the connections up to Paddington in the
morning were extremely poor. One mainly ended up
in Worcester Foregate Street.

Therefore, by rejection, this left the L.N.W. Coalport
branch from Wellington, where the trains never connected
with London trains, and the Much Wenlock branch from
Wellington. On this latter I found one station which
fitted so many topographical and railway facts that I
plumped for it—Buildwas. It means a change of trains at
Wellington. So you have to swallow the fact that Wodehouse never indicates that any passenger from London to
the castle by train had to change *en route*. And you have to
allow that, though Buildwas station was closed by the
'stream-lining' of British Rail in 1963, Wodehouse, living
in America, might never have been told so.

Substitute Buildwas for Market Blandings and consider
the facts arising. It is in Shropshire. Two and a half
miles from the station takes one to the lovely village of
Leighton where the Severn could run through the castle's
grounds. And it is 10 miles from the centre of Shrewsbury
—say 45 minutes without hurrying in the 1920s.

OR

The castle could be on the south side of the river, up the
slopes towards Much Wenlock. The Wrekin is terribly
close and, if the castle is on the south side of the river, and
therefore on a north-facing slope, every window must look
out at the Wrekin. But if it is on the north side and more
underneath the Wrekin, then I would expect there were
trees in the park which would hide the view unless you
climbed higher in the castle, i.e. onto the battlements.
Therefore I favour the former site. (N.B. This is the only

topographical fact that makes me favour the river between Coalport and Bridgnorth, but I cannot reconcile trains on that piece of line.)

I feel sure that Wodehouse would have looked into a *Bradshaw* at some stage, having settled on his area, and discovered at what times the trains went to London and back, and how long they took. I think he will have noticed the L.N.W. branch to Coalport and seen Madeley Market station. Could that have been a part reason for naming the station for the castle 'Market Blandings'? If only the trains had connected at Wellington, that would have been a fine station for his castle. (Could anyone have considered that Blandings Castle was really Apley Park? The Wrekin would be ideally 'visible from its battlements', and the Severn bounds miles of its park.)

Omitting the London trains for the moment (they are dealt with later), the following railway facts have to be reconciled:

Stops at, or first stop, Swindon: first stop Oxford. These two do *not* fit. They can be explained away, but that is not an answer. Never could one have gone from Paddington to 20 miles or so from Shrewsbury via Swindon. One could have gone via Oxford, but not have got farther north than Bridgnorth in the time taken.

Norfolk. A 1240 goes towards, and one returns about 1945. One can get to Yarmouth at 1946, leaving Buildwas at 1040 and return on the 0900 from Yarmouth, via Birmingham, arriving at 1751. Or, if one goes direct and does not mind changing many times, one can arrive at 2011. Inconclusive. Bridgeford to Market Blandings has branch-line trains taking half an hour. It is noticeable that Bridgnorth in the 1930s was between 26 and 29 minutes away from Buildwas.

Going into the daily services to and from London in

depth leaves much confusion of detail, though a general pattern emerges. I have chosen *Bradshaws* of 1910, 1932, 1939, and 1961 to cover the dates of publication of the various books. I have divided the books into three eras: 1915–1923, 1932–1939 and 1947, 1961–1976. Rightly or wrongly I have taken the publication date of each book to represent the date of the story in it. I put 1947 with the 1932–1939 era because I feel Wodehouse would not have been able to lay his hands on a war-time or post-war *Bradshaw*.

The DOWN Trains

Wodehouse has trains, in general, leaving Paddington at around 0830, 1118/1145, 1242/1250, 1400/1423, 1515/1615 and 1700/1705. I would equate these to the 0910, 1110 (there was also an 1115 and an 1120 in 1939) and 1400. His 1515 (1939) is, I suspect, his own inclusion, and the 1700/1705 he has, for his own convenience, equated with the 1610, for there is nothing between the 1410 and the 1610 (he states there is nothing between the 1400 and 1705 [1935]). His 1700 has a restaurant car; in 1910 the 1655 had a Dining Car, though the 1610 of later years had only a Tea Car.

The UP Trains

Wodehouse has a 'business-man's' train leaving variously between 0820 and 0850 and arriving at Paddington about midday. In fact there is nothing between the 0700/0720 from Buildwas, arriving Paddington 1100/1110, and the 0840/0913 arriving 1315/1408, so I think he has added this train, again for his own convenience. It connects with the actual 0855/0900 from Wellington which arrives in Paddington between 1205 and 1215 (from 1932 onwards). His other morning trains generally fit the timing of actual trains. His afternoon trains of 1400 and

1910 BRADSHAW

DOWN	Paddington	Buildwas
	dep. 1125	arr. 1528
	1415	1814
	1655*	2149
	* = Restaurant Car	

UP	Buildwas	Paddington
	dep. 0734	arr. 1215
	0913	1408
	1027	1500
	1210	1720
	1346	1820
	1517	2050

P.G.W. 1915–1923

	Paddington	Market Blandings
	dep. 1250	arr. 1500 (mistake)
	1615 express	?
	1700*	2105

	Market Blandings	Paddington
	dep. 0850	arr. 1200
	1050	?
	1445 ('the afternoon train')	?

1932 BRADSHAW (1939 in parentheses where different)

DOWN	Paddington	Buildwas
	dep. 0910	arr. 1403 (1408)
	1110 (1105)	1528 (1533)
	1410	1751 (1757)
	1610 (1605)	2004 (2011)

UP	Buildwas	Paddington
	dep. 0715 (0720)	arr. 1100
	0852	1405
	(1040)	1620)
	1203 (1200)	1700 (1705)
	1345	1800
	1515 (1520)	2005
	1804 (1802)	2205

P.G.W. 1932–1939 and 1947

	Paddington	Market Blandings
	dep. 1242	?
	1400 ('best train of the day')	?
	1445 express	?
	? express	1843
	1515	?
	1700	2105
	1705 ('nothing between the 1400 and this')	?

	Market Blandings	Paddington
	dep. 0820	arr. 1200
	0825	?
	1115	?
	1240	before 1700
	1400	?
	1445	?
	1800	?

1961 BRADSHAW

DOWN	Paddington	Buildwas
	dep. 0530	arr. 1151
	1110	1545
	1410	1820
	(No connections of 0910 and 1610 from Paddington.)	

UP	Buildwas	Paddington
	dep. 0700	arr. 1110
	0840	1315
	1155	1600
	1310	1715
	1802	2215

P.G.W. 1961–1976

	Paddington	Market Blandings
	dep. 0830	arr. ?
	1118	?
	1145	?
	?	1610
	1433	?

	Market Blandings	Paddington
	dep. 1035	arr. ?
	1240	'before 1700'
	1800	?

NOTES:
1. Wodehouse states 'a fast train takes about 3 hours 40 minutes'. In 1932 the 1410 took 3 hours 41 minutes.
2. Wodehouse states 'the 1400 is the best train of the day'. From 1910 to 1961 the 1410 (or 1415) down was throughout the fastest service of the day.

1445 agree with the actual 1345 and 1515, and the 1800 is exact with the actual 1802 or 1805.

It is clear that Wodehouse consulted *Bradshaw*, or that he had a railway-oriented person to give him the information—a general system of trains approximately two hours apart, up and down, which he then made to fit in with what he wanted.

I would prefer to have had positive confirmation that his passengers changed trains on their journeys up and down, but I believe that the sum of the evidence yields the conclusion that Buildwas was his Market Blandings.

*

Colonel Cobb was wise to take the publication dates of the books as giving the only possible time-scale to the enquiry. Although in this novel, *Sunset at Blandings* (1977), Galahad says he has only been gone a week since the activities of *A Pelican at Blandings* (1969), there are no years, or even months, specified in any of the books. There is a cold east wind at the beginning of *Something Fresh* (1915), and the house-party is strangely placed 'between the hunting and the shooting seasons'. Otherwise surely it is always high summer with the roses out, tea on the lawn, coffee after dinner on the terrace or in some garden arbour, bathing in the lake every day. Occasional thunderstorms, occasional showers and Lord Ickenham one time has a fire in his bedroom. Hammock weather otherwise, and a perpetual *annus mirabilis*. Oh yes, the Empress has now won prizes at Shrewsbury three years in succession. But, if you're going to be fussy about that, what price the information, in *Something Fresh*, that Lord Emsworth had been at Eton in the 1860s? No, stick to the publishing dates like glue.

Thank you, Colonel. The newly published *Oxford Literary Guide to the British Isles* by Dorothy Eagle and

Hilary Carnell, has no references for Blandings Castle or Wodehouse. We will be surprised if the second edition does not, on the strength of your identifications, have entries under these *and* Buildwas, Leighton and Madeley Market.

NOTES TO THE TEXT

1. Wodehouse, generally through the voice of Galahad, often calls Blandings Castle a Bastille, sometimes Devil's Island.
2. Would a Scotland Yard detective call the Chancellor of the Exchequer 'Sir James'? No, he'd have said 'Sir', and Wodehouse would have known this, by heart and ear, if he had lived more in England. When he wrote this, he had been nearly forty years away from England. (His own accent showed no trace of American.) In the typescript of *Sunset* he is writing 'somber', 'behavior', 'demeanor' etc. But he wouldn't have spelt them that way in a letter to England. The typescripts of his books went first to his American agent for duplication and sending out to publishers. His English publishers would make the alterations of spelling for the English market. In my early copy of the English edition of *Leave it to Psmith* (1923) I find 'arbor' and 'arbour' in different chapters.
3. The fact that Lady Diana's first husband was (a) handsome and (b) named Rollo makes one sure that she was lucky that he was eaten by a lion. In Wodehouse, as a general rule, all male Christian names ending in 'o', such as Cosmo, Orlo, Orlando, Rollo (not Pongo, Boko, Bimbo or Bingo — they were nicknames), stamped a man as being a wet or a sponger or a fool. It is strange, though, that when *The Clicking of Cuthbert* (1922) was published as *Golf without Tears* in New York in 1924, in the story 'The Long Hole', Ralph Bingham had been changed to Rollo Bingham. Hugo (as in Hugo Carmody) is the only acceptable male Christian name with an 'o' at the end.
4. Wodehouse's best girls (e.g. Stiffy Byng, Nobby Hopwood and Bobbie Wickham) certainly dominate their loved ones (The Rev. 'Stinker' Pinker, Boko Fittleworth and 'Kipper' Herring). It looks as though this last novel might almost have amounted to a reverse message to all mankind:

'Dominate her. She'll love it, and you.' Two of the major
characters in the Wodehouse novels have been Lord
Ickenham and Lord Uffenham, frequent advisers,
generally unasked, of timid young men. Their advice is
the same: 'Go to the girl you have been nervously and
distantly adoring, grab her like a sack of coals, waggle her
about a bit, shower kisses on her upturned face and
murmur passionate words (e.g. "My mate!") into her ear.
This seldom fails.' It got Cyril McMurdo, the ardent
policeman, a slap on the face first time from old Nannie
Bruce in *Cocktail Time*, but it brought good results in the
end. In this novel, *Sunset at Blandings*, Florence is surely
going to be reconciled to her 'weak' husband, but, equally
surely, only when she has seen him rise and dominate
someone—herself, one hopes. Lord Emsworth achieves
good results when he rises and dominates Florence and her
hanger-on, Brenda. They are so surprised and annoyed
that they leave the castle.

5. The Pelican Club, in Denman Street, Soho, was short-
   lived (1887–1892) but fondly remembered: by Galahad,
   who had been a prominent member, in Wodehouse's
   books, by Arthur Binstead in *A Pink 'Un and a Pelican* and
   Pitcher in Paradise, and by J. B. Booth in *Old Pink 'Un Days*.
   For a scholarly and suggestive analysis of the cousinship
   between the Pelican and the Drones, see a paper 'The
   Real Drones Club', by Lt.-Col. Norman Murphy in the
   August 1975 issue of *Blackwood's Magazine*.

   The Gardenia Club (see p. 22), in Leicester Square,
   was one of many started when the Licensing Acts of the
   1870s made restaurants close at 12.30 a.m. The Gardenia
   was a dancing club and, unusually, had women as well as
   men as members. It was less exclusive, in that way and
   generally, than the Pelican. It was opened, probably in
   1882, by the Bohee brothers, black musicians who had
   come over from America with Haverley's Minstrels. They
   sold the club to William Dudley Ward, father of the
   Member of Parliament for Southampton (1906-1922).
   Dudley Ward persuaded La Goulue (see Toulouse
   Lautrec's Moulin Rouge drawings) to appear at the club.

He sold the club to an Australian, 'Shut-Eye' Smith, who was its owner when the police closed it down, probably for infringements of the drinking rules, probably in 1889. I am indebted for this information again to Col. Murphy.

6. Jno Robinson has been the owner-driver of the Market Blandings station taxi (see picture, page 187) since *Heavy Weather* (1933).

7. This paragraph, almost word for word, is repeated from Chapter 2 of *Galahad at Blandings*. The end of the last sentence, about Galahad's policemen friends, is new.

8. When Beach, in his pantry, was being suborned by Ronnie Fish to help him steal Lord Emsworth's pig, Empress of Blandings, he put a green baize cover over his bullfinch's cage lest it should be shocked by what it heard (*Summer Lightning*).

9. Clearly this means that the action of *Sunset at Blandings* (1977) follows that of *A Pelican at Blandings* (1969) by a week. *Heavy Weather* (1939) followed *Summer Lightning* (1929) by a fortnight.

10. Beach has been butler at the castle since *Something Fresh* (1915), when he had an under-butler, Meredew. But now (1977), and in several post World War II books, he calls it eighteen years, and for all we know he would have called it eighteen years at the time of *Something Fresh*. Wodehouse has never treated time with anything other than irreverence. It shows that time does not quite stand still for Gally when he says that he is fed up with London. We have always seen Galahad as a deep-dyed Londoner, seldom far from the bars and barmaids, theatres and clubs of the West End: essentially a visitor to, rather than a resident at, Blandings. In *Full Moon* (1947), Gally said that he had never been able to understand his brother's objections to London, a city which he himself had always found an earthly Paradise. Now we know that, though he still has rooms in London, he regards his family home, in spite of sisters on the premises and Sir Gregory Parsloe across the fields, as his home and 'as near resembling an enchanted fairyland as dammit'.

11. Lady Diana, with Lady Florence still to come. This gives

Lord Emsworth and Galahad ten sisters at last count.
Wodehouse had a pleasant devil-may-care attitude to the
Threepwood sisters. On page 50 Gally can count up only
five sisters, and those include the newcomer Diana.
Wodehouse would have checked and corrected this
number before publication. Nine times out of ten
(literally) Wodehouse's purpose in dragging in sisters is to
provide 'heavies', people to boss Lord Emsworth, dis-
approve of Gally, say 'No' to lovers of daughters and
nieces. Lady Florence and Lady Diana have never been
mentioned before. And for the first time the benevolent
old author has given us a Threepwood sister whom we can
like. But she speaks no word and never comes onto stage.
The roster of sisters now and, alas, for ever, is: Lady Ann
Warblington [*Something Fresh*]; Lady Charlotte (what was
her married name?) ['The Crime Wave at Blandings'];
Lady Constance (first Keeble, now Schoonmaker. Both
her husbands have been American millionaires, both
nicer than she deserved) [*Leave it to Psmith*, *Summer
Lightning*, *Heavy Weather*, *Blandings Castle*, 'The Crime
Wave at Blandings', *Pigs Have Wings*, *Service with a Smile*,
Galahad at Blandings, 'Sticky Wicket at Blandings', *Plum
Pie*, *A Pelican at Blandings*]; Georgiana, Marchioness of
Alcester [*Blandings Castle*]; Lady Hermione Wedge (who
looked like a cook and whose daughter Veronica was the
dumbest blonde of all) [*Full Moon*, *Pigs Have Wings*, 'The
Crime Wave at Blandings']; Lady Garland [*Full Moon*,
Pigs Have Wings, 'The Crime Wave at Blandings']; Lady
Julia Fish [*Heavy Weather*, *Summer Lightning*]; Lady Jane
(what was *her* married name? Geoffrey Jaggard in
Blandings the Blest deduces 'Allsop' via *Galahad at Blandings*.
Perhaps. Her charming daughter Angela was the one
whose fiancé, James Belford, produced for the distracted
Lord Emsworth the wonder-working hog-call that got
the Empress back to eating properly ['Pig-Hoo-o-o-o-ey!',
Blandings Castle]; and now Lady Florence (Wodehouse in
his notes seems undecided whether it should be Moresby,
Ormsby or Appleby) and Lady Diana Phipps, soon to be
Lady Diana Piper, wife of the Chancellor of the

Exchequer. She was the only sister Galahad approved of. He disliked all the others and they disliked him. He had said to Lord Emsworth in *Galahad at Blandings*, 'I've always said it was a mistake to have sisters. We should have set our faces against them from the outset'.

12. Wodehouse had scored out a last sentence to this first paragraph of the chapter. It read, 'And this had always struck him as odd, for his sister Florence, her mother, had even in childhood been constructed of aristocratic ice'. Wodehouse took it out, probably, because Florence wasn't Vicky's mother, but step-mother. But 'constructed of aristocratic ice' is too good to lose.

13. Dolly Henderson married Jack Cotterleigh of the Irish Guards, and their delightful daughter (Sue Brown was her stage name) married Ronnie Fish, son of Galahad's sister Julia (*Summer Lightning* and *Heavy Weather*).

14. It is only in the last three Blandings books that the eighth earl of Emsworth, father of the current ninth, of Galahad and of ten daughters, gets more than a mention, and he is shaping up to being retrospectively, rather a nasty character: here, 'a bully and a tyrant'. It is odd that the benign Wodehouse dragged the eighth earl from his grave to make an ogre of him. If you try to work out when the ninth earl succeeded to the title, you must take into account that Vicky says she just remembers the eighth and he terrified her.

15. See *Full Moon* and *Galahad at Blandings*.

16. Lord Emsworth is still trying to get his beloved Empress painted for the Portrait Gallery at the castle. This quest was a strong strand in the plot of *Full Moon*, and there, too, the portrait painter came in under the assumed name of Messmore Breamworthy. Galahad, in that story, also told Lord Emsworth that his name was Landseer.

17. Eastbourne on the east coast? No, south, and 62 miles further west along the south coast is the town of Emsworth, on the Sussex/Hampshire border.

18. At this stage in the novel Dame Daphne Winkworth does not come nearer than being a voice over the telephone (page 100). But that enables her to puncture Jeff's alias at

Blandings. She has just sacked him as drawing master in her school even as, in *Galahad at Blandings*, she has sacked little Wilfred Alsop, the piano teacher. Dame Daphne, who has appeared in two previous novels, is one of the few links (Sir Roderick Glossop, the loony-doctor, is another) between the worlds of Bertie Wooster and Lord Emsworth. She was prominent in *The Mating Season*: widow of an historian, godmother of Madeline Bassett, mother of Gertrude, whom Catsmeat Potter Pirbright loves and courts. Her mother wishes Gertrude would be loved and courted by rich Squire Haddock, but Squire Haddock loves and courts Catsmeat's sister, Hollywood star Corky Pirbright ('Cora Starr').

Dame Daphne is described by Bertie Wooster as 'a rugged light-heavyweight with a touch of Wallace Beery in her make-up'. When Bertie and Esmond Haddock drink a large decanter of port together after the ladies have left the dinner table, and are 'discovered' by Dame Daphne waving the empties and singing a hunting song, she emits a memorably described four-letter word:
'Well!'

There are, of course, many ways of saying 'Well!' The speaker who had the floor at the moment— Dame Daphne Winkworth—said it rather in the manner of the prudish Queen of a monarch of Babylon who has happened to wander into the banqueting hall just as the Babylonian orgy is beginning to go nicely.

Curiously, in *The Mating Season*, 'she used to be head-mistress of a big girls' school'. But in her next two scriptural appearances she *is* a headmistress. In *Galahad at Blandings*, she has a small and unpleasant son, Huxley. She seems to have been thought to have been an early flame of Lord Emsworth's (not that Lord Emsworth can remember anything of the sort). It is now his sister Constance's idea, and briefly Dame Daphne's, that she ought to become Lord Emsworth's second Countess. (He has been a widower for twenty years.) Lord Emsworth is strongly against the whole thing, not least the idea of being Huxley's step-father. Huxley teases the Empress and tries to let her out of her sty for gallops in the meadow. He gets his deserts when the Empress bites him in the leg. His mother overhears Lord Emsworth telephoning the vet to make sure that the Empress can take no harm from this biting of the beastly boy. Any prospect of romance between Dame Daphne and Lord Emsworth after that is dead.

19. Claude Duff and Gally, after their chance meeting, ending so cordially, seem to have separated. We would like to know how, and would surely have been told when the typescript had been finally revised for print.

20. Fortnum & Mason (which I have always supposed to be Wodehouse's recurrent 'Duff & Trotter') tell me that a raised pie is made as follows: pastry, lightly cooked, is moulded round, or raised up, a wooden mould. The mould is removed and the pastry then filled with meat, usually game or pork, and the contents closed over with pastry again. The pie is then baked and served cold after a savoury jelly has been poured into the top to surround and seal off the meat.

21. Second son of Lord Emsworth, originally a sore trial to his father. But then he married the daughter of an American millionaire (she is a 'sort of cousin', too, of the Blandings head gardener, McAllister) and rose to great heights in his father-in-law's dog-biscuit business in America. Freddie's father is glad to have him married and a success and, especially, far away in America. At his first appearance, in *Something Fresh* (1915), Freddie is described as 'a heavy, loutish youth'. But in later books it might seem as though he had taken Slimmo and 'come over all slender' (*Full Moon*, 1952). He started as an ass and he remains a bit of an ass. But at no time is he such an ass as his elder brother, the heir, Lord Bosham (see especially *Uncle Fred in the Springtime* (1939)).

22. Yes, Hermione Wedge was a Threepwood sister, and she would probably have been changed to 'Florence' in a final draft here.

23. 'Blandings Castle has impostors like other houses have

mice', Galahad has said on another occasion. Many of them have been introduced by him.

24. Ovens's pub, the Emsworth Arms (see picture, page 150) in Market Blandings, famed for its home-brew ale served at all times of the day or night, has been just off-stage from the very first Blandings book to this last. It is almost an ante-room to the castle. And its home-brew, taken in sufficient quantities, has changed many a man's mood as a hinge in the plots. It is strange that in this typescript here Piper seems to have escaped from his guardian Murchison. Stranger, because in Wodehouse's preparatory notes, Murchison is sitting in a corner of the bar, guarding the gloomy Cabinet Minister, as his duty is.

25. Wodehouse had had a classical education and he ought to have remembered that the Gorgon, in Greek mythology, turned people to stone, not ice.

26. This sentence is a good example of Wodehouse 'writing short'. He would, of course, have made much more, in later drafts of the action sequence here. After the Second World War, when the *Saturday Evening Post* was no longer serializing his novels, Wodehouse was sometimes asked, by other and lusher American magazines, to submit his novels for pre-publication as one-shotter's — a whole 70,000-word book to be carved down to 25,000 words for a single issue of the magazine. Wodehouse could do it, and he did it, for substantial rewards. But to the reader brought up on his 70,000-word point-to-points, these 25,000-word one-shotters read like five-furlong sprints: very good, but not Wodehouse's natural distance. The sixteen chapters of *Sunset at Blandings*, in the barebones form to which Wodehouse had brought them when he went into hospital, remind me of his one-shotters in pace and discipline. He would have had every intention of filling the chapters out and slowing the book down. He had every intention of living to his century.

27. The typescript is here scored out, and the handwritten correction is impossible to read. But a page of the notes provides an alternative, 'the older Mr. Bessemer's companies'.

28. Three times in these chapters Wodehouse equates a character's look of despondency with the Mona Lisa. And he has done the same, several times, in earlier novels. In *The Code of the Woosters*, it is clear that Bertie Wooster has learnt this piece of imagery from Jeeves. But Wodehouse, Jeeves and Bertie have got it wrong. Walter Pater's *Studies in the History of the Renaissance* had been published in 1873, and no doubt the passage about the sensuous Mona Lisa (which is in Quiller-Couch's 1925 *Oxford Book of English Prose*) was already, at the very end of the nineties and in Wodehouse's Classical Sixth days at Dulwich, being set to boys for scholarly rendering into Greek. My guess is that Wodehouse, having tackled the passage as a schoolboy translator, misremembered it and that for 'Hers is the head upon which all the "ends of the world are come",' he was substituting, 'all the sorrows of the world are come'. Neither in Pater's view, nor in that of any other published critic that I have come across, had 'Lady Lisa' a sorrowful countenance. It is odd that Wodehouse's misremembering should have persisted beyond 1934 when *Anything Goes* was produced on Broadway and in London. Wodehouse and Bolton wrote the book, Cole Porter the lyrics and music and it was in this musical that Porter's 'You're the Top!' was first sung, containing the lines:

> You're the Nile, you're the Tow'r of Pisa,
> You're the smile on the Mona Lisa . . .

29. We haven't heard of a croquet lawn (see frontispiece map 26P) at Blandings before. Clock golf, yes. Bowling green (26P), yes. Tennis courts (27Q), yes. But the croquet lawn is new. Gally says they didn't play croquet in South Africa in the days of his banishment. They do now, and they take it very seriously.

30. The song-writer is Noël Coward, and the song 'Mad Dogs and Englishmen'. This was a bit of rhyming that Wodehouse, himself a past master lyric-writer (he used the word 'lyrist') for the stage, very much admired.

31. Why can't he call Jeff 'Jeff'? He might be Jeff Smith. It's the surname, Bennison, which might remind Lord

Emsworth of the man (Jeff's father) who got away with thousands of pounds of his cash. But, again, why not 'Jeff'?

32. It is not a bit clear why Gally says that the job Jeff is after is to be Lord Emsworth's secretary. Why not to paint the Empress?

33. This is the first Bentley reported as belonging to the castle. We have seen an Antelope and a Hispano-Suiza in earlier books.

34. How did Jeff know about J. B. Underwood being notoriously popular with the other sex? Not clear yet.

35. The Bill Lister incident. See *Full Moon*.

36. Rooks' eggs are green mottled with olive. Bill-stamps are that violet-indigo-blue colour from ink-pads for rubber stamping, as on the backs of cheques.

37. Wodehouse, on his typescript, has a big cross against the next four lines of dialogue, and the word 'fix' scrawled big. I cannot see what difficulty he had to surmount here. But 'fix' in his language to himself meant 'Do it again and get it right'.

38. Blissful Blandings weather: hammocks by day and a warm moon at night! The Californian climate is normal for Wodehouse's England, especially in Shropshire. Changes in the weather are always purposeful, as on page 83 to get Jeff off the terrace and to the realization that he has been locked out. On page 53 we find that strong sunshine ('get the lady a large hat') is used to arrange an entrance. In an earlier Blandings book, *Heavy Weather*, a sudden downpour of rain drives the sundered lovers into each other's arms in a deserted cottage in the West Wood. In *Full Moon*, if you can believe young Prudence Garland, a fortnight of rain had driven Freddie Threepwood to propose marriage to his first cousin Veronica Wedge as 'a way of passing the time when bored with backgammon'.

39. Still this slur on Sir Gregory. His is the face at the window of the Empress's sty in *Summer Lightning*, *Heavy Weather*, *Pigs Have Wings* and one story in *Blandings Castle*. In another story in that book his is the face peering into the pumpkin frame. But had he really done anything worse

than bad neighbourliness to the Blandings lot? He has certainly 'lured' George Cyril Wellbeloved away from the curacy of the Empress, to take up the ditto, for more cash, of the Pride of Matchingham across the fields. And he has bought a great fat pig in Kent, named her Queen of Matchingham and entered her against the Empress for the Shrewsbury Fat Pigs prize. This (see *Pigs Have Wings*) is considered unsporting, but there is nothing against it in the rule-book, he claims. And, in the theft and counter-theft of pigs in that book, Sir Gregory is a laggard compared with Gally and his accessories, Penny Donaldson and Beach. 'Tubby' Parsloe had been a rip-roaring young man about town, though such a past is always to a middle-aged man's credit in Wodehouse (see Jimmy Piper here, and Gally himself; see also Lord Worplesdon). Gally may still bear rancour that the young, untitled Gregory Parsloe had nobbled his (Gally's) dog Towser in a ratting contest. But in his heart Gally must surely admire a man who has stolen Lord Burper's false teeth and pawned them in the Edgware Road, and has been thrown out of the *Café de l'Europe* for trying to raise the price of a bottle of champagne by raffling his trousers.

40. Flask of strong drink emptied into the Empress's food-trough. See *Galahad at Blandings*.

41. Lord Emsworth's favourite book is referred to in the texts variously as Whiffle's *On the Care of the Pig*, Whiffle's *The Care of the Pig*, *Whiffle on the Care of the Pig* and just *Whiffle*. It is published by Popgood and Grooly, and the true name of its author may remain one of the minor mysteries of English letters. Lord Emsworth had a shelf devoted to pig books in his library, we know. In *Summer Lightning* he was reading 'his well thumbed copy of *British Pigs*' and, later in the same novel, *Disease in Pigs*. We are not told the name of the author of either book. Then, in 'The Crime Wave at Blandings', Lord Emsworth is shown harrassed by his sister Constance, his niece Jane, his grandson George and his *bête noir*, Rupert Baxter:

Sighing a little, Lord Emsworth reached the library and found his book.

There were not many books which at a time like
this could have diverted Lord Emsworth's mind from
what weighed upon it, but this one did. It was Whiffle
on *The Care of the Pig* and, buried in its pages, he
forgot everything. The chapter he was reading was
that noble one about swill and bran-mash, and it
took him completely out of the world. . . .
This is the first mention of the book. It appears in several
subsequent passages, especially in *Uncle Fred in the
Springtime*.

Then, in 1965, in *Galahad at Blandings*, not only was the
man named Whipple, but it turned out that Galahad
knew him: Augustus (Gus to his friends) Whipple,
member of the Athenaeum. And Galahad had the nerve
to get the current young hero into the castle (to pursue
the heroine, of course) in the guise of Augustus Whipple,
the author of the great pig book. Then, again of course,
the *real* Whipple turned up, anxious to see the splendid
prize-winning Empress of whom he had heard so much.
And Gally got his brother to start writing Whipple a
cheque for £1,000 to cover his gambling debts incurred in
a poker game at the Athenaeum. At least, that was
Gally's story, and a mere £1,000 was nothing to Lord
Emsworth to help the man whose book he doted on. But
why was he Whipple? Neither of Wodehouse's publishers, in England or America, knows why the honoured
name was changed in *Galahad at Blandings*. In *A Pelican at
Blandings*, published four years after *Galahad at Blandings*,
it's Whiffle again, described as an orthodox thinker in
comparison with the unnamed author of the 'startling,
ultra-modern pig-book' *Pigs at a Glance*. And now, in
Sunset at Blandings, we have, literally, Wodehouse's last
word on the subject. The name of the author of the pig
classic appears twice in Wodehouse's own typescript. The
first time he is Whiffle. The second time it starts as
Whipple, and in Wodehouse's recognizable hand, the
two p's have been changed firmly to two f's.

42. Wodehouse's irreverent fondness for the law — policemen,
magistrates, Justices of the Peace and occasional young

barristers—is a constant and varied joy. He gives his J.P.s extraordinary powers of arrest, sentence and imprisonment, and they are not slow to use, or threaten to use, them. Doubtless Murchison of Scotland Yard, although strictly there as the Chancellor of the Exchequer's personal watchman, can pinch a man he finds climbing at night into a window of a house where his ward is staying. Possibly Claude Duff's solicitor is right: he, Claude, can shoot someone climbing into his window. Possibly, as early as *Something Fresh*, Lord Emsworth was exercising the normal right of a castle-owner and J.P. when, having heard things and people going bump in the night in his hall, he descended the stairs spraying bullets from his six-shooter. Bertie Wooster's tangles with Sir Watkyn Bassett, as magistrate, ex-magistrate and county J.P., can get him anything up to thirty days in the jug without, apparently, a court, a bench, a jury or any suggestion that Bertie can get a solicitor to defend him. In *The Girl in Blue* a J.P., Crispin Willoughby, is in danger of arrest and imprisonment for pushing the local policeman into the brook in which he daily dabbles his feet after his hours of duty. In *Pigs Have Wings* Sir Gregory Parsloe, J.P., of Matchingham Hall, threatens imprisonment for pig-stealing (the Queen of Matchingham) on Lord Emsworth (himself a J.P. and presumably sitting on the same bench as Sir Gregory), Galahad and butler Beach. A J.P. can be terrible when roused by the suspicion that his pig or cow-creamer is being stolen. Wodehouse's books are liberally endowed with policemen, magistrates and J.Ps. For these, and for his clergymen, we are especially grateful.

43. As this book goes to press, nobody has been able to identify this song with certainty. Guy Bolton said he remembered it, but not its title, writer, singer or show. The Bank of England informs us that Mr. H. G. Bowen was their Chief Cashier from 1893 to 1902, and would thus have had his signature on all their bank-notes during that period. None of the Guards regiments could find any record of it in archives. The Adjutant of the First or

Grenadier Regiment of Foot Guards surmised that the writer was not a Guardsman, since the Guards wear bearskins, not busbies. A letter to the *Daily Telegraph* produced fifteen replies (mostly guessing W. S. Gilbert or P. G. Wodehouse himself as the writer), but no answer. The Research Department of the Music Library of the British Library, the Performing Rights people and the B.B.C.'s Music Library were all put to work searching, but they were defeated. George Wood, O.B.E. ('Wee Georgie Wood' of music hall fame), with the help of Marion Ross as a researcher, claimed that the song had been written by George Simms (author of 'It was Christmas Night at the Workhouse') and Jay Hickory Wood (biographer of Dan Leno Sr. and writer of many 'books' for pantomimes) for Dan Leno as an interpolated number for the pantomime *Dick Whittington* at Drury Lane in 1898/9. But, according to the records, the pantomime at Drury Lane that winter was *The Forty Thieves*.

44. See *Leave it to Psmith.*
45. The last entry in the train time-table between Market Blandings and Paddington. See page 197.

NOTE TO THE AMERICAN READER

Richard Usborne has mentioned, in his Notes and Appendices, approximately thirty previous books written by P. G. Wodehouse. The passionate collector of Wodehousiana who has had access only to the United States editions of his works may be baffled by eight of the titles that are unfamiliar to him or her.

The explanation is simple. Mr. Usborne, an Englishman, was authorized by the Estate of P. G. Wodehouse and commissioned by the British publisher, Chatto and Windus, to undertake this job. Naturally, he wrote with the English reader in mind, so the titles he cites are always those under which the books appeared in England. The fact of the matter is, however, that for good reason or bad, Wodehouse's American publishers sometimes saw fit to change the titles (with Wodehouse's consent and cooperation, of course).

So if you fail to recognize any of the eight titles listed in the left column below, you'll find the corresponding American title in the right column.

ENGLISH TITLE	AMERICAN TITLE
A Pelican at Blandings	No Nudes Is Good Nudes
Right Ho, Jeeves	Brinkley Manor
Performing Flea	Author, Author
Jeeves in the Offing	How Right You Are, Jeeves
Summer Lightning	Fish Preferred
Something Fresh	Something New
A Gentleman of Leisure	The Intrusion of Jimmy
The Clicking of Cuthbert	Golf Without Tears

NOTE TO THE AMERICAN READER

Author, Author, although taken largely from *Performing Flea,* is substantially different, having had some material dropped from the original book and other material added.

All the other titles mentioned in Mr. Usborne's text were the same in both the English and the American editions.

SIMON AND SCHUSTER

NEW HANOVER COUNTY PUBLIC LIBRARY

Wodehouse, Pelham
Grenville, 1881-
1975.

Sunset at Blandings

DATE		

11/78

NEW HANOVER COUNTY
PUBLIC LIBRARY
409 MARKET STREET
WILMINGTON, N. C. 28401

© THE BAKER & TAYLOR CO.